"Surely you've got time for romance?"

Lucas was so close now that Jenny could smell the clean, male scent of him, feel his breath stirring her hair.

Incredibly, beautifully male, she thought, desperately trying to concentrate on the pattern of his shirt.

"Lucas," she began, determined to impose some control on herself. "I think we should go back to the inn."

"Not yet, Jennifer.... Lord, you're entrancing."

No one had ever said anything like that to her before, and she looked up in surprise—instantly caught and held by the spark in those silver eyes.
"Am I really?" she asked artlessly, too captivated by him to think of being wise.

"You're exciting, Jennifer Howe, such a fascinating blend—feminine, capable, strong and unexpectedly fragile...practical and a dreamer...."

Elizabeth Barnes lives with her husband and son near Boston, Massachusetts. She likes to see treasures from the past lovingly restored and was instrumental in helping restore the local nineteenth-century church after it was badly damaged by fire. Vintage cars are a long-standing passion of the whole family.

Books by Elizabeth Barnes

Don't miss any of our special offers. Write to us at the following address for information on our newest releases.

Harlequin Reader Service
P.O. Box 1397, Buffalo, NY 14240
Canadian address: P.O. Box 603,
Fort Erie, Ont. L2A 5X3

A VINTAGE AFFAIR

Elizabeth Barnes

Harlequin Books

TORONTO • NEW YORK • LONDON
AMSTERDAM • PARIS • SYDNEY • HAMBURG
STOCKHOLM • ATHENS • TOKYO • MILAN

Original hardcover edition published in 1990
by Mills & Boon Limited

ISBN 0-373-03158-0

Harlequin Romance first edition November 1991

A VINTAGE AFFAIR

CHAPTER ONE

HATEFUL man! Inwardly seething, Jenny turned her back on Ralph and walked away. It was just her rotten luck to have run into him so soon, she fumed. She hadn't been at the meet five minutes—only long enough to leave her truck and its attached trailer while she ran into the inn to register and drop her things in her small room—and already Ralph had made his presence known.

It wasn't fair! She'd had more than enough of him during all those months of promises and false good nature, during those last ugly moments of threats and anger. What she didn't need now was more of him; she certainly hadn't needed that little exchange, his derisive, condescending stare, or the oblique warning contained in the few words he'd said to her.

It was enough to ruin the whole meet for her, enough to make her want to run up to her room and hide, but that was a luxury she couldn't afford. This had to be a working weekend for her. She needed to make contacts, drum up at least a little business by impressing people with the quality of her work. There was no use fretting about Ralph; it was time to unload her little car and begin.

Absently responding to the greetings of those who knew her, she hurried across the lush green lawn, cutting through the lines of beautifully restored antique cars already on display. Her rig stood waiting for her at the far end of the row of oldest cars; in just a few minutes she'd have her car parked among the others.

Reaching the truck, she first leaned into the bed behind the cab, lifting out her heavy tool-box and placing it on the ground at her feet. As she straightened up again, her muscles screamed in protest. No wonder, she thought, placing her hands against the small of her back, stretching to work free the kinks. It had been a long and tedious trip. She was feeling decidedly stiff after all those hours behind the wheel, all those hours spent worrying about the business.

'Hard trip?' someone asked from directly behind her, the voice unknown to her but low-pitched and attractive. Not a bit like Ralph's rough tone, she registered, relieved. 'You look beat.'

'Not really.' The denial was instinctive as she turned, hands still braced against her back, to find a stranger watching her. But not just watching, she realised when she moved her hands and his gaze followed that small gesture before returning to her face. Then, methodical and deliberate, he took the time to study each line and curve of her slight form, his expression knowing, speculative and slightly wicked.

'Do you mind?' she asked pointedly, because he was standing so close to her that he'd effectively trapped her against the side of the truck, unable to get to the trailer. 'I'd like to unload my car.'

'Your car? *You* brought a car?' She was briefly robbed of the power of breath when she saw his smile. It was devastating, and it went well with the glint of admiration in his eyes. Both the smile and the look were designed to tell her that he found her attractive in spite— or possibly because—of her faded jeans and old T-shirt. He was telling her that he didn't care that she was sticky and grimy from the long trip, that her hair was wild and wind-blown. He was being blatantly obvious as he let her know that he liked what he saw. 'Would you like me to unload it for you?'

'I unload my own car.' She glared at him, forcing herself to ignore the impact of his height, his emphatically broad shoulders and his long-limbed frame as she attempted to stare him down.

Finally, he stepped aside, but even when she turned away to unlock the trailer an image of him stayed in her mind. There was a craggy beauty about his face: patrician features with a weathered look, a network of fine lines at the corners of heavy-lidded eyes, slight creases bracketing lips which were definitely sensual when he smiled.

No doubt about it, she conceded, he was a handsome devil; all the more so because there was nothing slickly perfect about him. The lines helped, and so did a scar which slanted—pale against his deep tan—across his high forehead, catching the very edge of his cheek. One final touch, she reflected, one flaw to mar the perfection; it added an element of mystery or romance to the man.

Watch out, Jen! she cautioned herself. He's a lethal weapon, all charm and clever tricks—like Ralph, she realised with a sinking feeling. Ralph wasn't as smooth, and certainly not as good-looking, but they were two of a kind—Ralph and this stranger. They were the kind who spelled trouble. In her experience, most men spelled trouble, but Ralph was a stand-out in that category. She had a feeling that this stranger could be, too, and she wanted no part of him.

But he was going to be hard to discourage, she discovered when she pulled out the first ramp and found the stranger beside her. He reached for the other ramp, watching her to see how to lock his in place.

'Look, don't bother,' Jenny said through gritted teeth, drawing herself up to her admittedly less than impressive full height, again glaring at him. 'I don't need any help.'

'Yes, I can see that,' he agreed, the same appreciative glint in his eyes. 'You're obviously an extremely capable girl.'

'Then——'

'Why not take advantage of me?' he suggested, cutting off her attempted objection. 'What's wrong with making things a little easier for yourself?'

'Because——' Just like Ralph! Always trying to worm his way in, always wanting to be indispensable, she thought, seeing red. 'Because I don't want to.' It didn't take his quick grin to tell her just how silly and childish she sounded. Drat the man! she fumed, slipping into the trailer to work on the tie-downs which held her little car in place. 'Look, I like to do things for myself,' she tried again.

'And I like to be helpful.' Again, he'd stuck with her, edging his large frame into the trailer on the other side of the car.

It was airless and almost unbearably hot inside the trailer—surely that explained the sudden light-headed feeling that assailed her, Jenny decided. It had nothing to do with the fact that the two of them were alone in the shadowy darkness, or that the stranger dominated the small, enclosed space. In spite of the car separating them, he was too close, too potent, too attractive a force.

Even Ralph had never had this kind of effect on her, she realised, hurrying to release the tie-downs on her side. She wanted out, fresh air, and a greater distance between herself and this man.

On the other side of the car, he was working with easy efficiency, watching her as he had with the ramp, effortlessly duplicating her movements. He was good, Jenny allowed grudgingly. He'd either done this before or he was a quick learner, and he was considerably more graceful than Ralph. More good-natured, too, she conceded, almost against her will.

Faced with her rudeness and determination to work alone, Ralph would have taken it as a personal affront. By now, he would have turned stubborn and surly, overriding her objections with rough verbal force. With Ralph, there wouldn't have been any charm in evidence. He certainly wouldn't have grinned engagingly across at her as the stranger did now, when the last of the tiedowns was released.

'Now what?' he asked expectantly.

'Now I let off the brake,' she answered absently, too busy checking the alignment of the rear wheels to the ramps to remember that she owed this man no explanation, 'and then I push it out.'

'Or I do,' he suggested, continuing when she opened her mouth to protest, 'which isn't to say that I don't think you can. I *know* you can. You wouldn't be here on your own if you couldn't manage everything for yourself.'

'Then let me manage!'

'But think how it will look if I do,' he persisted, frankly teasing. 'Consider my image.'

'I don't care about your image,' she snapped, releasing the brake.

'No, I don't suppose you do,' he agreed cheerfully. 'There's no reason why you should, and no reason why you should refuse a little help either,' he added, the matter apparently settled to his satisfaction.

Which it was, she noted crossly. He'd already worked his way down to the end of the trailer; he was in the position to push and she wasn't. Short of an undignified scuffle, she didn't see any way to win this particular battle.

'All right.' She capitulated with a weary sigh. He'd got his own way, although she still hadn't worked out what he thought was in it for him. 'But push only on the wheels,' she cautioned, edging her way out of the trailer. 'If you push on the body, you could bend it.'

Outside, in the relatively cooler air, she drew a couple of deep and steadying breaths, only half watching as the car began to emerge from the trailer. Somehow she was going to get rid of this man, she vowed. She didn't have time for the kind of game he was bound to want to play. She'd played those games too many times, been hurt too many times. She wasn't about to get involved with this attractive stranger—or *any* man!—not after Ralph.

Ralph had been the worst, the most painful, the hardest to accept. Thanks to Ralph, she was older and wiser now. She'd finally learned the lesson that—at least with her—men were only nice when there was something in it for them. Whatever this stranger wanted—and it was probably only a weekend fling—she wasn't going to co-operate.

'Is this where you want it?'

She blinked as the stranger's words broke through her thoughts. Her car was off the ramps and tucked in at the end of the row. She nodded, a familiar feeling of mingled pride and delight coming over her at the sight of her car in the sunlight. At meets, it was always among the oldest and most toy-like; people were drawn by its bright red paint and gleaming brass.

Already, it was beginning to draw attention; she could relax now, she told herself. There was safety in numbers; the stranger was now nothing more than one of the crowd, and she was about to begin fielding the inevitable questions. She reached into the truck for her registration packet, took out the identifying placard and leaned it against one of the seats of the little car.

'Is it yours?' A voice spoke from the crowd, and when she nodded someone else asked, 'What is it?'

'A 1904 Franklin. They were made in Syracuse, New York from 1902 to 1934.'

'How fast does it go?'

'Forty to forty-five, if everything's running right. More, if I'm going downhill.'

'What's the horsepower?'

'Ten.'

'How many cylinders?'

'Four.'

'How much did it cost new?'

'About twelve hundred dollars.'

'What's it worth now?'

There it was: the same rude question, the one Jenny never answered. 'It's not for sale,' she said quietly.

'But if you did sell it, how much would you get?'

And what's your car worth? she was always tempted to ask, but never did. Politeness was part of her basic nature. 'It's hard to say,' she explained, going into her fogging routine. 'You see, so few like this ever sell that there's no established price. It's not like a Model T Ford, where a number change hands every year and you can at least know what the last few sold for.'

'Still, a car like this—one this old—must be worth a lot.'

'Not necessarily. Age is a mixed blessing.' She stopped as the crowd shifted slightly. Someone was now standing directly behind her, and it didn't take much genius to figure out who it was. Jenny could actually feel the stranger's presence. She knew, without looking, that he was watching her intently. Drat him! she fumed, her temper rising again. For a few minutes, she'd forgotten all about him, but it had been too good to last.

'A car this old is certainly rare,' she began again, picking up the thread of her previous comment, resisting the temptation to turn around and glare at the stranger, 'but it's harder to keep running—harder to find parts for it, and, without a top or windshield, driving isn't always fun. A lot of collectors don't want those kinds of hassles, which pretty much cancels out the value of its being rare. You see? There's no way I could put a price on it, and besides—since it's not for sale, I don't need to,' she finished brightly, repressing a smile as her questioner nodded and began to sidle away, a glazed look in his eyes.

'He's sorry he asked,' the stranger murmured in her ear, 'which is what you intended, isn't it?'

'You again,' Jenny said ungraciously, ignoring his question as she turned to confront him. 'I thought you'd gone.'

'If I'd left, I'd have missed your impressive lecture.'

'I wasn't trying to impress you.'

'But you did,' he assured her, smiling down at her, the spark of admiration still glowing in his eyes. 'It made you sound like an expert.'

'I am,' she answered shortly, wondering why, at a moment like this, she should suddenly remember how much Ralph had disliked the occasions when she'd sounded like an expert. 'It was a basket case when I bought it, and I did all the work on it myself.'

'What's a basket case?'

'A car that's all apart—a lot of little and not so little pieces. I thought everyone involved with antique cars knew the term,' she was pleased to point out. 'Aren't you in the hobby?'

'Afraid not.' He shrugged apologetically. 'My sister and her husband are, and they dragged me along this weekend. I've never been to a meet before, and I've been feeling out of my depth.'

Out of his depth? Ha! This man had never been out of his depth, Jenny thought, nor was he now. He had too much presence, the kind of authority that had already managed to isolate the two of them from the others gathered around her car, those people who just a couple of minutes ago had been busily asking her questions.

Out of his depth? No way! 'Or bored?' she suggested, because that seemed more likely.

'Not any more. Not since——' he paused, thumbs hooked through his belt, taking the time to survey her with appreciative deliberation '—not since a beautiful girl showed up with a beautiful car.'

Spare me, Jenny thought, closing her eyes. Even Ralph had never laid it on quite this thick! Of course, neither had he ever looked at her the way this man was looking at her... but that meant nothing, she hastily reminded herself. He was more attractive than Ralph, and he had a smoother line, but it was really all the same. He was after something—men were always after something—and it was time for her to bring this little encounter to a screeching halt.

'Yes, well...sorry to disappoint you,' she began, hating herself for her reluctance to do what she knew must be done. Fool, Jenny! she lectured herself. Won't you ever learn? '...but I'm afraid you're about to be bored again. I've got to go,' she finished abruptly, turning away. 'Find someone else to keep you amused.'

'All right,' he agreed equably, as she started to push her way through the people gathered around the car. 'I expect I'll manage—until you're free again.'

Of course you'll manage—but don't think I'll be free for you again, she thought, but didn't say. There was no point trying to get in the last word with someone like that. He was too smooth, too clever for the likes of her; she'd only lose if she tried. The only way to protect herself from this man was to put some distance between them, and to be sure she *kept* it between them!

'Jenny!'

She paused in the doorway of the inn, recognising the familiar voice hailing her. It was Tessa, perhaps Jenny's closest friend among those who regularly attended the same meets, although why she and Tessa should have become such good friends was beyond Jenny's comprehension.

Tessa was everything Jenny was not: tall and fair, an absolutely beautiful girl who knew nothing about antique cars and whose husband, John—a rank chauvinist, in Jenny's private opinion—liked it that way. John expected Tessa to be decorative and nothing more, and Tessa cheerfully obliged. In fact, Tessa was always cheerful, which was why Jenny enjoyed her company. In return, Jenny sometimes suspected, Tessa was grateful to have a friend who didn't treat her like a slow but attractive child.

'I'm so glad you're here,' Tessa called out and then, when she reached Jenny, she added *sotto voce*, 'and so is that incredible hunk who's been talking to you.'

'Making a play for me is more like it,' Jenny corrected, 'although I don't know why he bothered.'

'Don't sell yourself short,' Tessa advised with an assessing look. 'You're really smashing, in your own way—it's that dark and glowing gypsy air of yours. Obviously he's attracted.'

'I doubt that it's my gypsy air,' Jenny contradicted. 'I expect it's because he's on the prowl, and I'm probably the only unattached woman here this weekend.'

'Jenny,' Tessa countered with exaggerated patience, 'a man that gorgeous doesn't need to worry about whether a woman is attached or not. He could have anyone he chooses, and it's obvious that he's going to choose you.'

'Not if I can help it.'

'Oh, don't be like that! You could do with a fling,' Tessa decided positively, 'and with luck you'll find that your stranger is a kindred spirit, and the two of you will have a great time this weekend.'

'He's not *my* stranger,' Jenny countered, then turned to go into the inn. Talking to Tessa had only made things worse, she realised. Their brief conversation had forced her to acknowledge that a part of her wanted him to be her stranger, wanted to see a lot of him this weekend—which was madness, she reminded herself. She was here at this meet to do business, *not* to involve herself in a pointless flirtation! But what if it wouldn't be pointless? she found herself wondering as she went up to her room. What if this stranger really likes what he's seen of me and keeps on liking me? What if he's not like other men—not like Ralph? *If* he's different—and he *could* be!—wouldn't it be fun to find out?

But that's the way to get hurt, she cautioned herself when she'd finished her quick shower. If she let herself have a fling with him this weekend, nothing would come of it. He'd only be paying attention to her because no one more attractive and sophisticated was available. She obviously wasn't his type, she acknowledged, slipping into the pink and red print cotton dress, then pausing to inspect herself in the mirror.

Dark gypsy air indeed! she thought, rejecting Tessa's assessment. There was nothing special about Jenny Howe, she reminded herself, nothing to attract a man like the stranger—even if she did now look better than she had when she'd stepped out of the truck. The dress looked good on her, drawing attention to her slender waist before flaring out in a wild kaleidoscope of colours. The bright, bold pink and red suited her complexion and her dark hair—she'd known that when she'd bought the dress three years before, and she didn't think it looked too dated.

She was presentable, she concluded, setting to work on her hair, fussing until she'd subdued its wilful tendency to curl in all directions. When she was done, it lay smooth, only the ends curling softly to brush her shoulders. That's it, she decided, taking one last look in the mirror, wishing her face were more interesting, her almond-shaped eyes more exotic, wishing that stupid dimple didn't appear every time she smiled, or that——

Oh, stop it, Jenny! she told herself, disgusted. She had better things to do with her time than stare at herself in the mirror—as though she actually cared what the stranger thought of her! First she had to call her mother, who'd be worrying until she knew that Jenny had arrived. Then she had to forget about that man while she concentrated on making some business contacts.

There was no telephone in her slightly shabby little room in what had once been the servant quarters of the inn, so, armed with a fistful of change, Jenny went down to the pay phone in the lobby. Finally, when she'd deposited the right amount, she heard the phone ring only once before her mother picked it up.

'Jenny?' Alma Howe asked, and Jenny, hearing the threads of uncertainty and concern in her mother's voice, wished she'd called sooner. 'Are you there yet? Are you all right?'

'I'm fine, Mom,' Jenny assured her, investing her voice with an extra measure of confidence, trying to lend her mother some of her strength. 'The trip was no problem. How are you?'

'I'm all right, although the house seems awfully empty.' Her mother attempted a laugh. 'After all, it's the first time you've been gone since—— Well, I'll get used to that,' she finished bravely, but Jenny could hear the tears in her voice.

'Mom, you could have come. I wish you had.'

'Darling, I know, but I just couldn't, not without your father... But tell me,' she continued, brightening slightly, 'are you settled in yet? Met any old friends?'

'The car's unloaded——' no need, Jenny decided, to mention the man who had helped do the job '—and I took time to shower and change, but I haven't had a chance to really see who's here.'

'Not even Ralph?' Alma asked hopefully. 'He will be there, don't you think?'

Ralph! Thanks to the stranger—one point in his favour, Jenny was forced to admit—she'd forgotten all about Ralph. Now wild horses couldn't get her to tell her mother that Ralph was here. The last thing in the world she wanted was for her mother to get her hopes up. 'Mom, please don't start on Ralph again,' Jenny said, trying to be gentle as she evaded the truth. 'We've been through it before, and you know——'

'Oh, I know you don't like him any more,' Alma agreed, sounding wistful, 'but you did for a while. And he always liked you, and I can't help but think how much easier things would be now if you hadn't let him go. He'd be help for you in the shop, and you wouldn't have had to make this trip alone... It's just that he seemed so nice and helpful, and your father trusted him.'

Yes, but Dad was already sick when he hired Ralph, Jenny wanted to say but knew she could not. Dad had been ready to trust anyone who could take some of the responsibility from his shoulders, and—for once in his life—he hadn't shown good judgement when he'd hired Ralph.

But there was no way she could tell her mother any of this, Jenny knew. Alma was one of life's innocents. She'd gone straight from a loving family to her marriage with Jenny's father, and until his death he'd protected her from every unpleasantness. Jenny knew that her mother had no idea that there were unkind—even evil—people in the world, and now it was up to Jenny to shield her mother from the truth—especially the truth about Ralph.

'Mom,' Jenny finally attempted inadequately, 'it just wasn't working out.'

'I suppose not,' her mother conceded, sounding less than convinced, 'but I wish it could have. You and Ralph had so much in common, and he thought you were attractive—I know he did. You've got to admit, that's a big plus. So many young men are put off because you're——'

'—running a restoration shop,' Jenny finished for her. With that, they both laughed.

'I know, I'm a broken record, aren't I?' Alma offered apologetically. 'It's just that I'd like to see you settled and happy, married to someone who'd be good to you—as good to you as your father was to me—and Ralph seemed...well, I just hoped...It would have been lovely if Ralph had solved all our problems.'

If only her mother didn't believe that a man could solve all their problems, Jenny reflected when their call had ended. She could understand why her mother felt as she did—it made perfect sense to a woman who'd been married to Sam Howe for almost thirty years. But Jenny knew that her father had been one in a million; her chances of finding a man like him were close to nil—which was something her mother couldn't understand.

Not for the first time, Jenny found herself wishing she could confide in her mother. It would be grand not to be so alone with her problems, but the idea of burdening her mother with them was unthinkable. Sam's death had worked terrible changes in Alma, had almost destroyed her self-confidence and sense of security. To tell her mother just how bad things were might well crush her completely.

No, she couldn't talk—really talk—to her mother, Jenny concluded, depression settling on her like a pall. She was suddenly more discouraged than she usually liked to admit. This was one of those times when she felt terribly alone, when the dual tasks of trying to keep her mother on an emotional even keel and the business together were almost too much. This was one of those times when Jenny just wanted to quit, to give up the battle and——

No more of that! she sternly lectured herself. You can't let yourself feel this way. And she wouldn't, she resolved. She'd start mingling now, make some useful contacts and—most important—avoid both Ralph and that infuriating stranger.

The stranger, however, had other ideas, Jenny saw as soon as she reached her car. He was one of the admiring crowd gathered around it—he would be the tallest, she noted resentfully—and before she could turn away he was beside her.

'Haven't you got something better to do?' she demanded.

'You know I don't,' he told her, sounding amused. 'Since I got here, the only time I've had anything to do was when you let me help unload your car.'

'Let you? I had no choice.'

'Neither did I,' he murmured obliquely, then continued, 'By the way, I'm Lucas Lambert.' Before she'd realised what he intended, he'd extended his hand, taking hers in his firm grip. 'And you're...?'

It was a mistake to have let him touch her; she knew that immediately. Even a gesture this innocent was a mistake. He was too much of a presence, too overwhelmingly...physical, she decided, staring for a long moment at the hand enveloping hers. His was so large and so tanned that it made hers seem pale and delicate. Her mother wouldn't believe it, she reflected. She wasn't sure she did herself. 'I'm Jenny—Jennifer Howe.' The words were wrung out of her, almost against her will. 'People call me Jenny,' she added, finding herself curiously reluctant to withdraw her hand from his. To compensate, she fairly snatched it away, driving it deep into the pocket of her skirt.

'Jenny.' He nodded, ignoring her abrupt gesture. 'I wish you'd help me out.'

'How?' She eyed him with curiosity now that the contact between them was broken and she'd regained a bit of her poise.

'Well, cars aren't really my favourite thing, but my sister and brother-in-law are determined to get me into the hobby. I was taking a pretty dim view of their scheme, but now——' he glanced briefly at her car, then back to her '—I think I've found one that appeals to me, and, since you're the expert, I hoped you would tell me about it.'

She knew she shouldn't, but she'd already had a taste of the impossibility of saying 'no' to this man. Besides, a detached portion of her brain was forced to acknowledge, her resolution had already begun to weaken; it all but disappeared when someone in the crowd jostled her nearer to him. Now, standing so close, she found that she had to look up a considerable distance to meet his eyes. They were nice eyes, she decided: silvery grey, open and candid, not a bit like Ralph's.

'Please?' Lucas coaxed. 'It's a Franklin—I know that. Wes—my brother-in-law—says they're something special. He's got a later one, and thinks I should have one too.'

Oh, why not? Jenny asked herself. Surely it couldn't hurt to at least be polite. 'He's right—not necessarily that you should have one,' she qualified hastily, 'but they're definitely special.' She was on firmer ground now, launched on a topic close to her heart. 'They're not your average antique car. Franklins were always air-cooled and very well engineered. Aesthetically, the design is very good, particularly in some of the later cars—the Speedsters, for example, or the Pursuit and the Pirate.'

'All Greek to me,' he confessed cheerfully—another way he wasn't like Ralph, Jenny noted, remembering how Ralph had never been able to admit to gaps in his knowledge, 'and the last thing I want is a later car. I want something really old—like yours—something that's not much of a car.'

'Then you don't want one like mine,' Jenny countered quickly and proudly, and when she met his gaze she found him regarding her with lively interest and that same appreciative spark. Heavens! she thought, her heart suddenly beating faster. There was something about him: that smile and those silver eyes... 'My car is old, but it's not just a toy. It performs *very* well.'

'Does it?' he asked, his voice seductive, intimate, tinged with amusement, as though the two of them were sharing a very private joke. 'I suppose you're going to tell me it's a race car.'

'No, not that,' she conceded, returning his smile, 'but it does very well for an American car that old. If you want something that's not much of a car, you don't want one like this.'

'No?' He turned, eyes narrowed, to really study the car. Silently, he absorbed the high wooden spoke wheels and simple flaring fenders, the two black leather seats which were surprisingly like the bucket seats of a modern sports car, the arched engine hood with its intricate brass grill, the brass lamps mounted on brackets on either side of the dashboard. 'It's an absolute gem,' he observed after his lengthy inspection, 'but it looks like a toy. It's not very large, is it?'

'True.' At the moment, it seemed even smaller—dwarfed, really, by the presence of the towering figure beside her. 'But it's very light—the frame is wood and the body mostly aluminium, which cuts down on the weight and improves the performance.'

'Performance,' Lucas repeated with a sceptical lift of an eyebrow. 'I don't think of performance when facing a toy like this.'

'Toy' again, Jenny noted, wondering if he was baiting her, or was really as naïve as he sounded. 'Look,' she said, leaning in to pull the bonnet forward, revealing the engine. 'You see? Four cylinders when, for example, Cadillac had only one in 1904. That makes a difference.'

'Not much like today's engines, is it?'

'But a lot like the older Porsches and VWs.' Definitely naïve, she decided, convinced that she'd heard in his voice a note of doubt or uncertainty. 'The fins on the cylinders are for the air-cooling,' she explained, reducing the details to what she hoped was the simplest possible level. 'When the car moves, air comes in through the grill at the front of the hood and flows over the fins. It makes an excellent cooling system.'

To that he merely nodded—perhaps she was still being too technical, Jenny thought, repressing a smile—then he stooped, his long legs jack-knifed at the knees as he looked under the car. 'A chain?' he enquired, glancing up at her.

'It's called chain drive, like a bicycle,' she answered patiently. She could hardly get any simpler than a bicycle, she assured herself, but she was afraid Lucas didn't have a clue. He was obviously a mechanical babe in the woods! When it came to technical details, *she* was in control, and at least so far he didn't seem to mind that she knew so much more than he did. Maybe he *was* different; maybe this time would be different, she told herself, studying his thick dark blond hair with its sunstreaked highlights. Maybe this time would work... 'You see?' She knelt beside him. 'The chain runs from the engine back to the rear axle. It's a nice, simple way to transfer the power.'

'If you say so.'

'I'll show you, if you like,' she suggested impulsively. 'I'm always ready to try to convince a sceptic.'

He grinned, getting to his feet and extending his hand to her. Again, her hand was enfolded in his; she studied his long, tapering fingers, closed over hers. 'Are you offering me a ride?'

'If you're game.' Even when she was standing again, he didn't release her hand, a fact which made Jenny feel strangely breathless. 'Would you like one?' she asked, knowing that it would be wiser to withdraw both the invitation and her hand.

'Of course.' He maintained the contact between them a beat longer. 'I can't think of anything I'd like better.'

'Then we'll do it.' From her pocket she produced the ornate brass key, inserted it into the ignition switch on the coil box, set the spark and throttle adjustments, then reached for the crank. She gave a brief, apologetic thought to her mother, who believed that cranking the car was unladylike. Well, so be it, Jenny thought with a defiant toss of her head. This man was going to have to accept her as she was! With that much clear in her mind—if very little else about him—she inserted the crank, gave one strong pull, then a second.

When the car was right, as it was at the moment, it almost always started on the second pull, and now the harsh clatter of metal on metal shattered the silence around them. Deftly, she stowed the crank in the compartment under the seats, leaned over to turn on the oiler, then closed the bonnet. 'We're set,' she called to him over the noise. 'Get in.'

She used the step plate to climb up into the seat behind the steering-wheel, readjusting the spark as he went around to take the passenger seat. As soon as he was beside her, Jenny used the lever outboard of her seat to engage first gear, hearing the familiar slap of the chain against the frame and the high whine of the planetary transmission as the car began to move.

Instantly, she was in her special world. Driving the car had always been a joy, and ten years of practice had made her very good at it. Now the task absorbed her as she judged the engine speed, checked the traffic as they turned on to the highway, decided precisely when to shift into high.

The noise level dropped considerably, even as the speed increased. They were doing about thirty now, she could tell, and the wind was firm against her face, destroying all her careful efforts with her hair. And so what? she asked herself with a small smile. She wasn't trying to impress this man!

'You're certainly exposed to the elements up here,' Lucas said, leaning a little closer to her, so that his words wouldn't be snatched away by the wind. 'What do you do when it rains?'

'Stay home, find an underpass or a good leafy tree.'

'You're serious, aren't you?'

'Of course,' she assured him, her dimple making a fleeting appearance when she grinned. 'It's a small price to pay for the fun.'

'But it's more than fun,' he told her, and his answering smile was thoughtful—almost wistful, she decided, before turning her attention back to the road. 'It's another world, a better one—to feel the wind and sunlight, to smell the roses ... It's a special kind of freedom, isn't it?'

It was, of course, and she was pleased that he understood such intangibles. There was more to this man than she'd thought. She wasn't sure what to make of him, and, in the process of trying to figure him out, she thoughtlessly and quite automatically turned into the state forest not far from the inn. Not a bright idea, she told herself, although she'd often used the setting to show people how well her little car could perform. There were plenty of paved roads and rough dirt tracks, and never much traffic—a good place to put the car through its paces.

But today? With this man? she asked herself. A deserted state forest was a little too secluded. Bringing this charming stranger here was probably a mistake, but it was also tempting... *very* tempting!

CHAPTER TWO

BUT she wasn't personally tempted, Jenny assured herself. It was just that Lucas was more of a kindred spirit than she'd imagined; she wanted to show him how well the car could perform. Here, on the smooth paved road leading into the heart of the forest, she could run the car at speed, race against the wind with an exhilarating rush. Then, when the paving ended and the network of dirt roads began, she could show him just what the little Franklin's high clearance and full elliptic springs could do to smooth out the roughest track.

She saved her favourite spot for last, down-shifting to first to make the steep and winding trail up to the highest point in the forest. There, in the dappled shade, among a stand of pine trees, she cut the engine. Instantly, the silence was filled with the sound of the breeze sighing high among the pine boughs, and the air was heavy with their scent.

'There! Do you see—can you feel it?' she asked, so caught up in the mood and the moment that she forgot her brief doubts about bringing him to this deserted spot, her voice unthinkingly hushed so as not to break the spell. Impulsively, she turned towards him and caught the rapt, faraway expression in his eyes, and guessed that he had some idea. 'It's not just a car, a mechanical thing,' she explained when he finally focused his gaze on her. 'It's a way into a different world.'

'A world out of time...'

She nodded, leaning one arm against the wood and brass steering-wheel, her other hand resting lightly on the division between his seat and hers. No one had ever seemed to grasp it as clearly, as deeply, as he did. Now, far from being frightened or distrusting him, she was liking him a great deal. He understood what it meant to her! 'It's a world with more beauty in it. In this car I can always find spots like this and take the time to feel a part of the beauty. Time doesn't really matter in a car like this. It's been around for almost ninety years, so a few more minutes are always there—always time to smell the roses or the pine, to watch sunlight on a stream or listen to the wind.'

'To feel the contrast between shade and sunlight,' he offered with a smile.

'To find these secret places. It's a kind of magic...' And a kind of magic seemed to be growing between them, she realised, and suddenly she was afraid again, needing to break the spell. 'Come and see the view,' she directed, slipping out from behind the wheel and jumping to the ground. 'We've worked our way around until we're really not far from the inn. It's just a little way down the main road, and you can see it from here.'

In spite of the soft covering of pine needles beneath their feet, she could hear his footsteps following, and when he stopped just behind her her whole body was aware of—alive to!—his closeness. 'There.' At the edge of the bluff, where the ground fell steeply away, she pointed for him.

Below, beyond the forest, the ribbon of road ran back through fields and clusters of houses to where the steep roofs of the inn were visible among its own stand of trees. The lawn, where all the antique cars were gathered, was a glowing green, the cars merely toys, the people moving among them tiny, unreal figures.

'When I was little, my father used to bring me here,' she told him with a reminiscent smile. 'It always made me think of the train set he'd helped me put together in the cellar—miniature cars and miniature people, only these cars and people could move, while the ones at home just sat there. This was more fun.'

'Then you've been coming here for a long while?'

'All my life, or nearly so. My father had a restoration shop—I run it now,' she added on an unconscious note of pride, 'but even before he started the business, he had an antique and was a part of this group. The shop was just a way to combine business and pleasure—that and the fact that he loved working on cars and was good at it. We always went to a lot of meets, but this has always been one of my favourites—even now, when I'm back without him for the first time.'

'You must miss him.'

Jenny shrugged. 'Of course, and it hasn't been easy... Still,' she finished more briskly, refusing to permit her worries to intrude on this moment, 'I'm learning that there's life after you think the bottom's fallen out of things.'

'True. I've been learning that too.'

When she glanced up, she found his gaze unfocused, far away. Had something similar happened to him? Had the bottom fallen out of his life? Had his family suggested this meet as a kind of healing process for him? Perhaps it had something to do with that scar, still new, she thought. There was mystery here, and a question hovered on her lips.

Perhaps he sensed that, because he made a deliberate effort to focus his gaze on her, changing the subject. 'You must have been an interesting little girl—with a train set in the cellar.'

'I was my father's joy and my mother's despair,' Jenny confided with a grin, knowing her dimple was showing again. 'You'd have to call me a tomboy—heaven knows, Mom always has. I liked cars and model trains and being in the shop with Dad. I've never been what my mother wanted me to be, although she certainly tried hard enough to change me. It didn't work, and now she's decided that I'm beyond redemption.'

'Mother's wrong.'

He returned Jenny's smile, his own slow and lazy—definitely sensual, she decided, suddenly weak at the knees. Heavens! No man had ever made her feel this way before, certainly not Ralph, not even when she'd been thinking... But this was different, *very* different. *Anything* could happen now, she thought a little wildly.

'Are there moments you'd like to hold on to?' he asked in a different tone, finally breaking the silence—and the tension—between them. Reluctantly, she glanced up at him to find that he was admiring the car parked among the pines, the play of sunlight striking sparks off the well-polished brass. 'That's one I'd like to keep.'

'It could be 1904 again,' she agreed dreamily. 'There's nothing here to tell us that we're reaching the end of the twentieth century. It could still be the dawn of it, the world still innocent. We ought to be wearing different clothes and have a wicker picnic hamper with us, and be going home on all dirt roads, and meeting mostly horse and buggy rigs, and—and...' She faltered and then stopped when she saw his expression. While she'd been prattling on about the past, he'd turned to look at her, was staring at her with the intensity that had first warned her that he could be dangerous.

'Don't mind me,' she told him, instinctively retreating from her dream, starting briskly towards the car, only pausing when she already had one foot on the step plate. 'I get carried away sometimes, too caught up in the romance of it. Of the *car*,' she added pointedly. 'Only the car.'

'Why stop there?' he asked with a teasing smile. 'Why limit romance to the car?'

'Because——' She stopped, feeling cornered. Somehow, he'd managed to close the distance between them to stand very close to her. One hand was braced against the steering-wheel and his large form was blocking the sun.

'Because——' she tried again without conviction, torn between what she knew she ought to do and a strange new tangle of emotions: curiosity and longing and something even deeper. 'Because I don't like to be bothered by—by distractions,' she finally managed, wondering if the words sounded as false to him as they did to her. 'I don't have time for romance.'

'That's inconsistent,' he pointed out, still teasing her. 'I thought you said that this car was all about taking time. If you've got time to smell the roses and the pine, surely you've got a little time for romance?'

'No!' He had her trapped, his one hand still on the steering-wheel, the other resting on the padded leather of the seat, imprisoning her within the small space created by the circle of his body and his arm. 'Please...' she began again '...I shouldn't have brought the subject up. I wouldn't want you to think...'

'Wouldn't you?' he asked with another of those devastatingly intimate, sensual smiles. 'Why not?'

'Because——' Damn! There was that word again—that weak and nothing word, when she was never at a loss for words. But Lucas was so different from any man she'd known before—different and dangerous. He was a far too potent blend of power and sensitivity; he could destroy her with the force of her attraction to him. Perhaps he already had, she acknowledged. Now that he was so close, she could smell the clean male scent of him, feel the heat of his body, feel his breath stirring her hair.

Her legs were suddenly weak, and to steady herself she took her foot off the step plate, only making things worse. Now he was an even more towering presence, and intensely male. She tried staring fixedly at his shirt and the carefully matched plaid of the fabric, but out of the corner of her eye she could see his arm, braced against the steering-wheel. The muscles were well defined, the smooth dark skin dusted with a sprinkling of fine golden hairs... Incredibly, beautifully male, she thought, desperately trying to concentrate on the pattern of plaid. 'Lucas,' she began again, determined to impose some control on herself, 'I think we should go back to the inn.'

'Not yet, Jennifer... Lord, you're entrancing.'

No one had ever said anything like that to her before, and she looked up in surprise. Instantly she was caught, held by the spark in those silver eyes. 'Am I really?' she asked artlessly, unable to do the sensible thing and look away, too captivated by him to even think of being wise.

'Oh, perhaps not to every man's taste,' he teased with a grin which brought back the creases to bracket his mouth, 'but to mine, certainly. You're exciting, Jennifer Howe, such a fascinating blend—feminine, capable, strong and unexpectedly fragile... practical and a dreamer.'

'That sounds nice,' she breathed, completely under his spell. He was going to kiss her, she guessed, her heart beating faster as a mixture of fear and wild excitement swept over her. She wanted him to kiss her, but she wanted even more than that. She wanted things she'd never wanted with any other man, things she hadn't known before. There were feelings inside her that were either new or had been waiting for this moment and this man. She wanted to be absorbed and possessed by him, wanted him to draw her completely out of herself and into a world where time and reason and logic didn't exist... 'Mother wouldn't believe it,' she said on a note of wonder.

'Mother's wrong,' he told her again, still smiling, his silver gaze still holding hers, 'but then, she doesn't know you the way I do.'

Jenny blinked, cold reality back with a vengeance, the madness of the last few minutes completely gone. 'Lucas, we don't know anything about each other.'

'I know a great deal about you,' he contradicted gently, 'and you know me better than most people do.'

'I don't know you at all! You're a stranger.'

'You think so?' he asked, a new note of reserve in his voice. 'Well ... perhaps for the moment, at least, it's better that way.' Without warning, he placed his hands at her waist, lifting her off her feet to set her in the driver's seat of the car. 'Miss Howe,' he said in a complete shift, playing the game of being very proper, very respectful, 'will you drive me back to the inn?'

'I——' She stopped, hating herself. This was the wise thing to do, wasn't it? This was the safe thing, so why did she feel disappointed? 'If that's what you want?'

'It's what you want,' he reminded her, 'and what I suppose I want, too—at least for the moment.' He bent to open the compartment behind her feet. 'You keep the crank here—I was watching,' he told her, opening the door to produce it. 'If you tell me what to do, do you think I'm capable of starting the car?'

'I suppose so,' she answered, quelling her disappointment as her hands moved on the spark and throttle levers, taking great care in their adjustment. 'You put the crank in there.' She leaned forward to show him.

'Now what?' he asked expectantly when he'd inserted the crank.

'Now you change the way you're holding your hand,' she explained. 'You don't want your fingers on one side of the handle and your thumb on the other. If the engine kicks, that's a sure way to break your arm. Put your palm on the crank handle, and keep your thumb and all four fingers together, then push hard... Yes, like that.' She nodded, watching while he tried and the engine almost caught. 'Now, once more,' she instructed.

This time it did catch, the clatter destroying the silence of the pine grove. 'Very good,' she called to him, her good humour restored when she saw the glint of proud satisfaction in his eyes. This man *is* different, she assured herself, even as she shifted her feet so he could stow the crank back in the compartment under the seat. He's not having fun at your expense, he's not using you, and he's not a predatory master craftsman of romance! At least... he may be a master craftsman, but he's not a predator. He's different enough not to grab a kiss the first chance he gets, and lord knows you gave him more than a chance! You gave him the most open invitation a woman can give a man, and he didn't take you up on it.

Instead, he acted like a gentleman and gave you some time. What was it he said? ' ... at least for the moment.' Well, for now, he hasn't kissed you, but he *likes* you! He thinks you're exciting and a fascinating blend... and he *will* kiss you some time!

'Well, I've got that much learned,' he observed cheerfully, the little car shifting slightly off centre when he climbed into the seat next to hers. 'Nothing to it.'

'Not as much as most people think,' she agreed, favouring him with a brilliant smile, not even stopping to think that her dimples were showing. This was almost too good to be true—that he liked her and liked her car, that he liked learning about it and didn't mind having her as a teacher!

Spirits soaring, she engaged low gear and started down the rough track, pushing the car to its absolute limits, shifting into high just as soon as she could. Almost a downhill slalom for cars, she thought absently, concentrating on the bends in the track, loving the way the quick steering obeyed her commands. At the bottom of the hill, she took the sharp left turn at maximum speed, knowing that people unfamiliar with the car always grabbed for something to steady themselves against the alarming sway.

But Lucas didn't, she saw when she risked a quick glance. Better and better, she thought, turning her attention back to the road, her mind still imprinted with the image of his hands resting lightly, completely relaxed, on his knees. He was even more of a kindred spirit than she had thought: sensitive, but not averse to a little excitement and challenge.

'What do you think?' she asked when they were back at the inn, her voice unnaturally loud in the silence created when she'd killed the engine. The lawn was nearly deserted now, the slanting rays of the sun telling her that most people would either be in their rooms changing for dinner or already gathered for cocktails on the back terrace. 'Do you still think my car's a toy?'

'No. It's something very special.' He half turned towards her, his arm resting on the division between their two seats. Deliberately, he brushed back an errant curl from her temple, his fingers briefly warm on her skin. 'Thank you, Jennifer, for sharing something that matters so much to you. You've let me into a very special world with your car, and, much as I never thought I'd say this about an automobile, I'd like to stay.'

'Stay?'

'Yes, stay in that world.' He smiled, a slow, reflective and private smile, his eyes briefly far away. 'Sorry,' he apologised after a moment, focused on her once again, 'but for reasons that would take longer to explain than we've got right now, I could use something like this.'

'What do you mean?'

'That I've become a convert. My family think I should have a car like this, and you've showed me *why*. I'm convinced. I want into your world—the world your little car offers...so meet me in the lobby in an hour, and I'll start my campaign.'

They parted at the top of the first flight of stairs, Lucas going towards the front of the inn while Jenny turned into the labyrinth of corridors at the back. There's the difference between us, Jenny Wren, she told herself, reality returning with a crash. He's got one of the nice rooms at the front, and you're stuck away at the back. He's got money; you haven't. You've been on a high, thinking how much the two of you have in common, but there's a world of difference, too, and best you not forget it. *Don't* get your hopes up! This is just a weekend meet, after all, and the two of you aren't likely——

'Well, finally—here's Jenny! You're a hard girl to track down.'

Turning into the last dim corridor leading to her room, Jenny jumped a mile, instinctively stepping back a pace as Ralph Porter materialised, hard by her door. Even without their earlier contact, when his warning had been clear but unspoken, his presence here would have alarmed her. Feeling as she did about Ralph, it had been bad enough to face him outside in the sunlight, with dozens of other people around. Here, in this shadowy and deserted corridor, it was worse.

It had taken Jenny a while to realise it, but there was a menacing quality about Ralph. He was only a little taller than she, but solidly built—almost, but not quite, stocky—with an aura of raw and crude power about him. He wasn't bad-looking, but there was a lack of refinement in his rough features, and his eyes had always bothered her. They were cold and shrewd, well-suited to anger, yet Jenny had been exposed to that anger only once.

But once had been more than enough, and she shivered as she remembered his towering rage on the day she'd told him to leave. Now, of course, he was smiling, but it was a bitter and insolent smile which didn't reach those cold, shrewd eyes. This was not going to be pleasant, she told herself, fighting to control the sick sinking feeling in the pit of her stomach.

'What's the matter, Jen?' Ralph enquired, still smiling. 'You don't seem very happy to see me.'

'I'm not,' she answered, standing her ground, refusing to retreat any further back down the corridor, but equally unwilling to produce her key and open her door—not with Ralph standing beside it! 'You know how I feel about you.'

'Don't I just?' He laughed softly, then instantly sobered. 'You made it clear enough, that day you sent me packing. An attitude like that could give some an inferiority complex, but not me, Jen, and do you know why? It's because I've always got a plan in my head, some way to keep an edge.'

'But we're through, Ralph—done with each other, so there's no way you can keep an edge on me.'

'But I can, Jen. I did, starting right after Sam died, when I made my pitch and you turned me down. You were nice enough about it, but I could tell which way the wind was blowing. From then on, there was no use thinking I might marry into the business——'

'Don't flatter yourself,' she snapped, clinging to the remnants of her pride. 'There was never any chance of that.'

'Oh, I don't know,' Ralph reflected. 'We got along pretty well for a while. You liked me, Jen—you know you did. You were pretty well stuck on me, I'd say. I think you'd still be liking me, maybe even would have married me by now, if I hadn't made my pitch too soon.'

'Never,' she told him with an expression of distaste, ignoring the partial truth of what he'd said as she remembered the day when, as he'd put it, he'd made his pitch. It had been soon after her father's death, and Ralph had come at her—there was no other way to describe it, nothing subtle about Ralph! He'd mauled her with his rough hands, asking her to marry him and telling her to sign the business over to him—all in the same breath. It had opened Jenny's eyes to the reality of Ralph in an instant, and in that instant all the friendship and easy camaraderie she'd thought they shared had been destroyed. Still, she'd tried to hide her shock and revulsion. She'd thought—fool that she was!—that she still owed Ralph something for the load he'd carried during her father's illness, that she still needed his help in the shop.

She'd refused to marry him with all the politeness she could muster, and they'd continued working together in an uneasy truce, pretending nothing had happened between them. It hadn't been until that last day, when there simply hadn't been enough money for Jenny to continue paying his salary, that she had learned exactly what Ralph thought of her... 'I'd *never* have married you,' she told him now, her voice shaking with the strength of her emotion, 'not if you'd been the last man on earth!'

'Easy enough to say now,' he observed with a cunning smile, 'but you didn't feel that way until the day I asked you. When you turned me down, I knew that I'd blown what could have been a good thing. I wasn't going to get the shop that way, so I knew I'd have to find some other way. That's when I started planning.'

'Planning what?'

'Ask me into your room,' he suggested smoothly, 'and I'll tell you about it.'

'Are you crazy?' she demanded. 'There's no way I'd invite you into my room!'

'But it's not for the usual reasons,' he explained, still smiling. 'You're attractive enough, but that's not what's on my mind now. No, I just thought the time had come to tell you about the tricks I played on you—make you understand why you should accept the business offer I have for you.'

'What—what kind of tricks?' she asked, instantly wary.

'Invite me into your room and I'll tell you. It's not the kind of thing I care to discuss out here, where someone might be listening.'

'I'll bet,' Jenny responded coldly, her expression giving no sign that she was weakening. She didn't care about his business offer, but could those tricks he'd mentioned be the reason why the business was dying on the vine? She *had* to know! 'All right,' she finally agreed, producing her key and fitting it into the lock, 'but if you try anything, I'll scream my head off.'

'Don't worry, Jen. I'm only after the business.'

'I already knew that.' She waited until he was inside, then closed the door and leaned against it. 'So tell me about these tricks.'

He nodded, taking the only chair. 'Dirty tricks, I think they're called,' he remarked after a moment. 'Once things went sour between us, I knew my days were numbered, that you'd find some way to get rid of me as soon as you could, but that didn't stop me wanting to take over the shop. If I couldn't marry into it, I figured I could pick it up for a song if business went bad. It would take a little longer, of course, and cost me something, but a dying business comes cheap, and I knew I could afford something. The trouble was that I didn't want to wait too long or pay too much, so I decided to tinker just a bit, to speed things along.'

'What did you do?'

'Little things.' He shrugged, his face bland and expressionless. 'Those last two engines we worked on together—I put in the main bearings, in case you've forgotten, and I put in the wrong ones. Those two engines are already causing trouble, so I hear. In fact, one's already thrown a rod. You've got two unhappy owners right there, Jen, and another two who have fresh paint jobs already beginning to fade or chip. Remember that little blue Buick we did? And the bright red Stutz? You did a lousy paint job on both of them.'

'*You* did the paint job on both of them!'

'And doctored the paint, but you can't prove it, any more than you can prove that I did all the work. Besides, the work came out of your shop—it's your responsibility. No, Jen, the word is already out that you don't know what you're doing. When Sam was alive, he kept you from making mistakes, or corrected them before the work left the shop, but now that he's gone... Well, you're just not good enough. Your work can't be trusted—at least that's what I hear.'

'But how...' she began, feeling sick, wondering how she'd missed seeing what he was doing '...how did you manage it?'

'Very easily.' Ralph smiled complacently, self-satisfied, expansive. 'You never bothered to check my work, did you? You might have stopped trusting *me*, but you still trusted my work, and that was your mistake. All I had to do was tip the scales in my direction and wait for you to throw in the towel, but you're so damn stubborn that you haven't done it as soon as I thought. That's the only reason why I'm telling you now—so that you'll finally realise that you don't stand a chance. The word's gone out on you, my girl: your work's no good, and there aren't many people who will give you more. A few, maybe, but not enough to keep the shop going—not if you and your mother want to eat. As far as you're con-

cerned, the business is gone, but I'll make you an offer—
not a very good one, but you can't expect me to pay top
dollar for a place that's failed. What do you say, Jenny?
Are you ready to sell to me now?'

'I'll see us both in hell before I sell to you,' she hissed,
her mind working frantically. 'I'll get in touch with those
four owners and tell them I'll make the work right for
free. I'll get my reputation back!'

'You can't do that. You haven't got the cash,' Ralph
pronounced flatly. 'The one dumb thing Sam did was
to not buy enough life insurance. From the minute he
died, you were cash poor, and I figure that you must be
just about out by this time.'

'Then I'll get a loan.'

'Who'll loan to you?' Ralph asked derisively. 'You
don't have any credit, and no sane person would advance cash to try to save a business that's already gone.
No, Jenny, you'll have to sell to me.'

'I—I'll do *something*,' Jenny countered distractedly,
panic warring with the cold germ of an idea. Could she
do it? she wondered wildly. Then, remembering her
afternoon with Lucas, the half-formed idea became
whole. 'I'll sell my Franklin,' she announced, more to
herself than to Ralph. 'That will give me the money I've
got to have... You see?' she continued, now speaking
directly to him. 'You haven't won, after all!'

'Well, that's a debatable point,' he observed ju-
diciously, not in the least disturbed by her show of defiance. 'I figured you'd think of the car, so I'm prepared
to help you out with it. I've got a buyer for your little
car—a fat cat, willing to pay top dollar and even more.
You won't get a better price than my man is prepared
to pay.'

'And there's a good finder's fee in it for you, I
suppose.'

'Of course,' Ralph acknowledged blandly, 'but what the hell, Jen? This way, you get what you need to at least try to save your shop.'

'And you're selling my car for me out of the kindness of your heart?' Jenny asked with bitter sarcasm. 'You're willing to forget about buying the shop, while you help me out?'

'Not exactly. I'm not getting the shop—not *yet*, at least,' Ralph explained complacently, 'but I'm getting the next best thing. I'll have given my fat cat what he wants, and he'll be grateful to me, grateful enough to help me out in a lot of ways. I'll have my finder's fee, too, so I'll have that much cash behind me if you still can't make a go of the business and decide you have to sell. You see, Jen? This way we both win.'

'But I won't sell through you,' Jenny snapped, her rage getting in the way of good judgement, not caring how much Ralph's buyer was prepared to pay, 'so you don't win a thing. I'll find my own buyer, and I'll use the cash to fix those four cars. You lose, Ralph. You're out in the cold in spite of your planning. And,' she added, stepping away from the door to open it, staring pointedly at him, 'you're out of here. Get lost!'

'For now,' he agreed without argument, pushing himself up out of the chair, 'but I won't stay lost forever. Sooner or later I'm going to win, because you don't have all the time in the world to sell that car, and my man has cash in hand. You'll have to come to me, Jen,' he warned, pausing briefly in the doorway, taking a moment to brush his knuckles across her cheek. 'I'll see you around.'

'Not if I can help it,' she retorted as he strolled off, then she rubbed her hand furiously against her skin, trying to erase his touch.

CHAPTER THREE

'NOT if I can help it,' Jenny repeated, drawing a deep breath when Ralph was gone, 'and you don't know it yet, but I'm pretty sure I already have a buyer for my car.'

Just as he'd promised, Lucas was waiting for Jenny, leaning casually against the wall in the lobby. Lucas— Lucas Lambert, the man who would buy her car, Jenny thought, then her heart skipped a beat or two and she briefly forgot all about Ralph.

Lucas really was an incredibly attractive man! He'd been watching the stairs for her, and when he saw her his smile began: a slight, appreciative turning of the corners of his mouth. Then the smile broadened to reveal strong, even teeth, a brilliant contrast to his deep tan.

And this tall, blond god actually found her attractive, Jenny thought with wonder, even as she continued lightly down the stairs. The proof was there in the way he smiled and the way his eyes followed her progress, the way he straightened up and came to meet her as she reached the bottom step.

'Am I late?' she asked breathlessly, staring up at him.

He shook his head. 'Don't worry about it. You're here. That's all that counts.'

'I got held up,' she started to explain, and in that moment the memory of Ralph and all he'd said to her intruded. 'I——' She hesitated, knowing what she had to do and wishing she could avoid the task. It wasn't that she hated the idea of selling her little Franklin, although in other, more nearly normal circumstances, the very idea would have brought her pain. Now her only regret was that business had to intrude, that Ralph was going to make her spoil what might have been a perfect evening. 'Lucas,' she began tentatively, and his eyes narrowed, studying her face. 'I don't suppose—that is, you sounded as though ... Would you like to buy my car? It's for sale,' she finished more firmly.

'You don't mean that,' he told her, then took a moment to study her even more closely. 'Do you?'

'Yes.'

'But why? Jennifer, that car means so much to you.'

'I need money,' she said frankly. 'I've got to sell to someone, and the first chance goes to you. Do you think you want to buy it?'

'First, I think we'd better talk. Jenny——'

'Jenny,' said Tessa at the same moment, materialising to favour first Jenny, then Lucas, with her best smile. 'You're going to join me for dinner, I hope—you and——' She paused, waiting expectantly.

'Tessa, this is Lucas Lambert,' Jenny explained. 'Lucas, my friend, Tessa Harmon.'

'Well, hello, Mr Lambert.' Tessa extended her hand, at the same time subjecting him to a careful inspection. 'Have I seen you somewhere before?' she asked innocently.

'I doubt it,' Lucas said, sounding impatient, Jenny thought. 'Perhaps earlier today?'

'Perhaps,' Tessa agreed, still all innocence. 'You two will have dinner with us, won't you? John's off somewhere, talking cars, and if he remembers I'm here he'll want to keep on talking cars, so I'd love——'

'Sorry, but Jenny and I have some business to discuss,' Lucas interrupted smoothly. 'We were just on our way out.'

'Oh.' Tessa stared hard at him for a moment, opened her mouth, then closed it again and stared some more. Probably wondering if his intentions are honourable, Jenny thought with amusement, or if I'll be safe with him. But he apparently passed Tessa's inspection, because she finally smiled. 'Well, then, don't let me keep you. Nice to have met you, Mr Lambert.'

'We don't have to go out,' Jenny said when Tessa had moved away.

'Yes, we do,' Lucas responded almost grimly. 'This is too important to discuss here, where we'll be constantly interrupted. Come along,' he urged, taking her hand. 'We'll go into town, find someplace quiet.'

He hurried her out of the inn, down the path to the lower car park. 'My car's over here,' he directed, his hand resting briefly, warm, on her arm.

Heavens, a very black V-12 Jaguar Saloon—as the British would say—Jenny thought, blinking twice, impressed. She liked nice cars, and this one had an undeniable air of breeding: conservative, but with performance implicit beneath the refinement. At least she didn't need to wonder if she'd put Lucas on the spot when she'd offered to sell him her car. Any man who could afford a V-12 Jag surely had enough to acquire a new and expensive toy.

For someone who hadn't a mechanical clue, he drove very well, she noted, half turned in her leather seat, watching him. His hands rested easily on the steering-wheel and he shifted with neat precision, driving at a sedate and legal pace. A reasonable, rational man, she decided, surprised to discover that she felt completely comfortable with him. In fact, she was really looking forward to spending this evening with him, unless——

What if he took her somewhere *too* elegant, where she'd be out of her depth? A man like Lucas Lambert obviously could afford the best and no doubt knew how to behave in the kind of place that would be all *haute cuisine* and starched *maître d'*—not exactly her strongest suit. Besides, she wasn't dressed for that kind of evening; the cotton dress she'd thought looked very good this afternoon now seemed decidedly tacky and second-rate—particularly in the company of a man who drove a V-12 Jag and wore a Rolex! The whole evening, she decided with a sense of foreboding, was about to be ruined. She'd feel gauche and out of place, and whatever rapport she and Lucas had achieved would be gone.

But she needn't have worried. The place he chose in the fishing town down the coast was an unpretentious old building on one of the harbour wharfs. There was a deck on the water, people as casually dressed as Jenny enjoying quiet conversation against the sound of gulls and the occasional drone of a fishing boat heading in with its day's catch.

'So,' Lucas began when their drinks had been brought to their small table, 'why are you suddenly selling your car?'

'I told you.' She shrugged, fiddling with the stem of her wine glass. 'I need the money.'

'But that begs the question. Why do you need the money?'

'It's what's known as a cash-flow problem. At the moment, I've got to spend more than I can take in, so I need an infusion of cash. That's something I learned in a business course.'

'Jargon,' he observed, dismissing her explanation with a brief gesture. 'It still doesn't tell me why.'

'Do you need to know all the details?' she asked with a little heat. 'I wasn't aware that knowing why the seller is selling was a customary condition of sale.'

'Of course it's not customary,' he agreed, regarding her over the rim of his glass, 'but I thought we were already a long way beyond what's customary. Jennifer, you love that car; it matters to you. How are you going to feel—about *us*—if I take it away?'

About us. She'd been staring down at her wine, but she had to look at his face when she heard those two words. Was there already an us? she wondered, and when she saw the steadiness of his regard and his careful, watchful expression she decided that there must be.

'You can't *take* what's freely offered,' she pointed out, but she knew that wasn't the issue. 'Do you—do you really want to hear all about it?'

'Absolutely.'

Absolutely—a word with a nice clear meaning, with a wealth of strength and purpose behind it . . . like Lucas himself, she realised. Even so, she didn't tell people her problems—that wasn't her way!

'Why stick on this point?' he asked softly, reading her thoughts with uncanny accuracy.

'Because.' She shrugged, her resolution already beginning to weaken. 'It's a long, dreary story.'

'I've got plenty of time.' He smiled, leaning back in his chair to get comfortable, as though he'd stay there all evening, if that was what it would take. 'Don't stop now.'

'All right.' She capitulated, again fingering the stem of her wine glass while she wondered how to begin. 'I've been running the restoration shop since my dad died, but the business has dwindled to almost nothing. I knew I'd lose some work because there are men who don't trust a woman to work on their cars, but I couldn't understand it when things got *this* bad.'

'Especially as you'd been working with your father for several years, hadn't you?' Lucas queried, and it was obvious that he'd heard at least some of her story from someone else—not surprising, Jenny knew, given the way people loved to gossip at meets. 'Surely you'd been building a reputation of your own.'

'Not with some people,' she explained, now anxious to talk, finding that it was a relief to finally confide in someone, 'but that's not the real problem. I had this fellow working for me, and...well, he and I had our differences, and then money got tight, so I had to let him go. But I'd never have thought...' She stopped, took a sip of her wine, then forged on. 'It's hard to believe, but Ralph came to see me after our ride——'

'Ralph?' Lucas asked quickly. 'This fellow's name is Ralph?'

'Yes. Ralph Porter,' Jenny told him, staring down at her glass, trying to contain the hot anger rising again, 'and he told me that before I let him go, he sabotaged four of the cars we worked on together. Now the word is out—and I know he's doing everything he can to spread it around—that it was all my fault, and that none of my work can be trusted.'

'How did he do it?' Lucas demanded.

Heavens! He sounded almost as angry as she felt, Jenny realised, and found herself momentarily distracted, wondering if he could possibly care that much about her. *Could* he, after knowing her for only these few hours? It made no sense, yet his feelings seemed clearly written on his face. His mouth had thinned to a hard line, causing a muscle to knot along the angle of his jaw, and his eyes had suddenly taken on a glint of cold calculation.

He was on her side! Incredible as it seemed, she had to believe that she wasn't alone in this mess. Of course, Lucas couldn't actually do anything for her—except to buy her car and give her the money to fight Ralph, Jenny reminded herself, but Lucas's support was heartening. It stiffened her resolve, whipped her own indignation to an even higher pitch. Now she gathered her scattered thoughts and proceeded to tell Lucas exactly what Ralph had told her.

'The bastard,' he said with ominously quiet ve-
hemence when she had finished. 'Can't you prove what
he's done?'

'No. Ralph only sabotaged cars we'd both worked on,
so I can't absolutely prove what he did. Besides, if I
tried, it would only look like sour grapes, as though I
were trying to blame him for my own mistakes. Oh, I
wish,' she began, then lapsed into silence, brooding over
the injustice of it all.

'Wish what, Jenny?' Lucas asked softly, recalling her
to the present.

'I wish Dad had never hired Ralph, that he'd trusted
me enough to believe that I'd keep things going once he
got sick. The trouble was that his enlightened attitude
finally broke down.'

'His enlightened attitude?'

'His belief that I could run the shop every bit as well
as he could. Once he knew that I wanted to work in the
shop with him, he was all for it. He was convinced I
could take over from him—which, back then, we both
thought would be years away, when he'd decide to retire.
He even joked about changing the name to "Howe and
Daughter".'

'And your mother?' Lucas asked, amusement playing
across his features. 'She must have loved that!'

'Oh, she'd given up on me a long time before, except
for wanting me to marry...someone,' Jenny recovered
quickly.

'And how about you? Is there someone you want to
marry?'

'No, not yet, anyway,' she answered, her tone determinedly cheerful. 'I've never met anyone who mattered
that much, and I haven't had any real offers,' she added
in a burst of confession. 'I intimidate most men.'

'You don't intimidate me,' Lucas pointed out with
another of those devastating smiles.

'I don't expect anyone intimidates you,' she told him. 'You're not most men...but that's beside the point,' she added hurriedly, suddenly afraid that she'd gone too far, anxious to get back on a safer track. 'We're here to see if you'll buy my car.'

'How is selling the car going to help fix the mess Ralph has made?' Lucas countered promptly. 'Or are you just selling it to raise enough money to keep things afloat for a little while longer?'

'No!' She stared across the table at him, shocked at the very idea. 'I need the money to tide me over while I repair the damage he did. I'll make up some story about defective parts or inferior paint, and offer to do the work gratis. That's the only way I can change people's opinion of me. There's a lot of talk in the hobby—a lot of old-fashioned gossip—and so far, Ralph has had it all his own way. But once I make good on the problems, that news will get around. People will begin talking about how I stand behind my work, and that my work is good after all. Then I'll finally begin to get more work, and, even though it will be tight for a while, I'll manage to save the business.'

'But why sell your car?' Lucas persisted. 'Why not just get a loan?'

'You don't think I haven't already tried that?' Jenny laughed, tossing her head. 'I've been short of cash for nearly six months, and when I went to the bank, you should have heard the loan officer on the idea. I am not a good risk. I'm a woman trying to do a man's job; I'm in an uncertain field; the business is already going downhill, and there's no use throwing good money after bad...and I have no collateral, nothing to use to secure the loan.'

'You can't take a loan on the shop itself?'

'I don't own the shop. I've got a long-term lease, and I can't borrow on that.'

'The car, then? Couldn't you borrow on that?'

'It wouldn't give me enough, even if I could borrow on it,' Jenny explained. 'I tried, thinking I might be able to patch something together, but my friendly loan officer explained that the bank does not give loans on speculative items—and he considers a 1904 Franklin to be a highly speculative item.'

'Then let me loan you the money.'

His words were so easy, so matter-of-fact, that for a moment Jenny wasn't sure she'd heard him correctly. 'You don't mean it,' she finally managed into the silence between them. 'You can't!'

'But I do. Why not, Jennifer? I've got it to spare, and I trust you.'

'You don't even know me!'

'I know more than enough. Your work is good; you're determined; you're not afraid of hard work. You'll make it, and I can't think of a better investment than that.'

'You're mad,' she burst out. 'You don't know any of those things! They all happen to be true, but you can't know that they are. We only met a few hours ago.'

'That doesn't matter,' he insisted stubbornly. 'I still know all I need to about you, and I want to invest in your business.'

'Well, you can't,' she said shortly. 'You may have money to burn, but someone has got to make sure you don't just throw it away.'

'And you've elected yourself to the job?' he asked, grinning.

'Somebody's got to,' she retorted. 'Look, the loan officer was right. A loan to me doesn't make sense, and I wouldn't let anyone make me a loan out of friendship or sympathy or . . . or——' Or what? she wondered. She could hardly add 'physical attraction' to the list, but that was what it *had* to be in this case! 'Or anything,' she finished lamely.

For a moment, afraid to meet his gaze, afraid she might have offended him, she stared down at her empty wine glass. 'No,' she finally began again, lifting her head to a stubborn tilt, 'I'm going to do this the *right* way. I don't want anyone's charity. I just want to sell my car.'

'Then I'll buy it,' he offered quickly, 'tonight, if you like. Shall I write you a cheque?'

'But are you sure?' she asked uneasily, beginning to feel that she might have backed him into a corner. 'You don't *have* to do this!'

'Yes, I do,' he countered firmly, but his tone was intimate and knowing. 'Jennifer Howe, I don't have any choice—any more than you do.'

'But you *do*,' she insisted. 'I don't want you to feel that you've been coerced into doing it.'

'Coercion has nothing to do with how I feel,' he told her, his words hanging in the air, his gaze holding hers for a long moment. Then he broke the spell by reaching into his pocket, taking out a leather-bound notebook and flipping it open. 'Now,' he continued briskly, producing a pen, 'we need a purchase and sale agreement.'

'But I'm not sure—that is, I hadn't quite decided what the price ought to be,' she temporised, beginning to feel that *she* was now being coerced. 'I'd only just made up my mind that I had to sell it, and——'

'That's all right. You can set the price later.' He bent his head and wrote quickly for a couple of minutes, finally tearing two sheets of paper from the notepad and passing them to her. 'There. Is that acceptable to you?'

'I don't know.' Doubtfully, she picked up the papers, noting the precise angularity of his script before she forced herself to focus on the words.

'I, Lucas Lambert,' the first one read, 'agree to purchase from Jennifer Howe her 1904 Franklin for whatever sum she shall specify.'

Below those few words, Lucas had signed his name with a flourish, then added the date.

The second one read: 'I, Jennifer Howe, agree to sell my 1904 Franklin to Lucas Lambert for a sum to be established by me.'

'Here. I've just written two more.' Lucas passed her two identical slips of paper, then handed her his pen. 'Now we'll each have copies. Just sign, and it's done.'

'I suppose so.' She drew a deep breath, then signed the first. 'Is this really legal?' she asked, looking up.

'Absolutely.'

There was that word again, she thought, and this time it made what she was signing seem very legal indeed. 'There,' she said when she'd signed her name to the second paper, sorting them out. 'Here are your copies.'

'Jenny? Are you really sure?' he asked urgently, not touching the slips of paper. 'I still don't feel right about this—you shouldn't have to sell your car because of what—this man has done. Why not the loan?'

'I've already told you why not the loan,' she answered calmly, feeling better about her decision with each passing moment. Lucas was the right person to have her car, and the deed was done. Besides, if things went according to the plan—the wild dream!—already half formed in her mind, the little red Franklin might not be entirely out of her life. 'Yes, I'm very sure.'

'All right, then...' After a moment, he picked up his two copies, carefully placed them inside the leather-bound notepad and returned it to his pocket while Jenny slipped her two into her purse. 'But there's one thing more,' he resumed, smiling across the table at her.

'What?'

'We've got to seal the pact.' His smile widened into a grin. 'In more normal circumstances, that would mean a handshake.'

'All right.' Obediently, she extended her hand.

'No, Jennifer.' He shook his head, even as he took
her hand into the reassuring warmth of his own. 'We're
miles past the handshake stage.' He leaned forward
across the table, the pressure of his hand compelling her
to do the same. 'This pact we seal with a kiss.'

'Here?' she asked unsteadily, feeling colour rush to
her cheeks. 'In front of all these people?'

'Why not? All they need to do is take one look at you
and they'll understand why I want to kiss you.'

'But...' she began, blushing furiously now, then
blurted out, 'Are you married?'

'Me? Of course not.' His clear silver gaze held hers,
lending reassuring weight to the casual words.

'Then it's all right,' she whispered, her capitulation
complete when he smiled at her.

'Of course it's all right,' he murmured. His lips
touched hers briefly, almost chastely, but the warmth
and the strength of his kiss sent a message to her, prom-
ising more. 'Now, it's time to eat,' he announced,
sounding enormously pleased with himself as he took
her hand and they went into the dining-room with its
exposed beams and dark panelling.

For all that the place was unassuming and casual, the
food was first-rate, and Jenny learned that Lucas was a
connoisseur of both food and wine. Deciding what to
order mattered to him; he was a man who knew his way
around the world, Jenny sensed. She was impressed, so
impressed that she dismissed the small, niggling fear that
she might be out of her league with a man like Lucas.

She was with him, wasn't she? He was there across
the table from her, watching her with those deep grey,
hooded eyes, the fine lines in the corners showing when
he smiled, the grooves on either side of his mouth calling
attention to the sensual curve of his lips. He was attractive, charming, amusing, clever...a Renaissance man,

she decided dreamily, then roused herself when he started to pour the last of the wine into her glass.

'No, you have it. I've had more than enough—more than you've had,' she said in mock accusation. 'I hope you're not trying to get me tipsy so you can have your way with me.'

'No, that's not my style.' He held her gaze for a long moment, the implication clear. If Lucas Lambert decided he wanted his way with her, he wouldn't need to get her tipsy to do it. 'Besides, I've got to drive home,' he added, tilting the bottle to drain the last of the wine into her glass, 'as soon as you're ready...'

Outside, after even the restrained murmur of other late diners, the silence was pronounced. It was late; the wharf and street beyond were deserted. Adding to the sense of calm isolation, there was fog coming in off the water. It seemed right not to disturb the stillness as they walked back to the car.

'Lucas?' Jenny finally felt free to speak when they were inside the car. 'We talked all evening, but only about me and my problems, so I know almost nothing about you. I don't even know what you do for a living.'

'That's because I'm not doing anything at the moment,' he answered easily enough, but he'd been about to put the key in the ignition and now he stopped himself. He sat, half turned towards her, fingering the key in a quick, nervous gesture. 'I was... involved in an accident almost two years ago. It's taken me some time to get over that.'

'And before?' she asked carefully. There was something here that troubled him, yet she sensed that he was waiting for her to pursue it. 'What did you do before that?'

The key went still between his fingers. He didn't speak for a few moments—Thinking? she wondered—then he shrugged. 'Nothing of any consequence.'

'Nothing?' There was a street lamp beyond the car, but its fog-shrouded light did little to reveal his profile. 'Nothing?' she asked again, feeling her way. 'But I can't believe—that is, you must have been doing something.'

'I had one of the longest delayed adolescences on record,' he offered into the silence, sounding grim and perhaps just a little self-conscious. 'I've spent the last ten years—since I got out of college—travelling...knocking around Europe most of the time. It wasn't very productive—just open rebellion against my father and all the things he wanted me to do. I'd probably still have been rebelling if the accident hadn't finally driven some sense into me...

'But now I've got to decide what to do,' he continued after another moment's deep thought, the key finally moving between his fingers again. 'I've got the rebellion out of my system, but I'm not sure what to do next.'

He leaned forward to start the engine, and Jenny studied the way his hair lay, curling slightly against the back of his neck, the way his shirt strained over hard shoulder muscles. 'There's the family business, but Wes—my brother-in-law—is running that now.'

'Your father?'

'Died two years ago, about the same time yours did, I should imagine,' Lucas supplied, guiding the car carefully through the thickening fog. 'He died without the satisfaction of witnessing even the start of my reformation. If he were alive, though, he'd still want me to go into the family business—something I still don't want to do. I couldn't make any particular contribution, for all that it's what I was trained to do, nor would I want to.'

'Why not?' she asked, thinking that the tables had certainly turned. Before dinner he'd managed to get her to tell him a great deal; now she was proving to be nearly as effective with him. 'What is the family business?'

'Precision engineering,' he answered, taking her questions in reverse order, his gaze never leaving the road as he spoke. 'It makes a lot of odd-ball parts for a lot of odd-ball equipment—mostly defence and scientific stuff. The trouble is that it's never involved with a finished product, nothing real. None of it interested me in the least, even though my father forced me to study engineering and draughting in college. He was determined that I'd take over the business; I was born to become the next son in Lambert and Son. But unlike you, Jennifer, that wasn't what I wanted. We fought about it all through my growing-up years and had one last big towering battle when I got out of college and announced my intention to...live in Europe. For a couple of years we didn't speak at all, but then Carole—my sister—married Wes. He came into the business, to do what I was supposed to have done. He had both the qualifications and the interest to do what I wouldn't, so my father was happy enough—although he never forgave me for...leading such a frivolous life. He was probably right. Heaven knows, I was doing it mostly to spite him.'

'But you must have liked it, at least at the start,' Jenny mused, trying to justify the meaningless lifestyle of this man she now liked and respected—and was strongly attracted to, she admitted reluctantly. They were out of town now, on the road back to the inn, still moving cautiously, and she stared out at the thick fog. Travelling, knocking around Europe, obviously having more money than sense—all typical playboy stuff, but she knew Lucas well enough now to believe that it just didn't fit. He *wasn't* a playboy!

'Now I wonder if I ever enjoyed it,' he said softly, proving her point, 'but I've still got to figure out what to do with the rest of my life...and Carole and Wes decide that I need a hobby, for goodness' sake!'

'Well, you just bought my car, so you've got one—like it or not. Perhaps it's a start.'

'Perhaps,' he agreed, sounding a little more cheerful as they pulled into the inn's car park.

The fog was much thicker here than it had been in town. It had blanketed the tall lamps along the edges of the car park and blurred the forms of the modern cars parked in their neat rows. The stand of trees between the car park and the inn had disappeared, and the small lamps along the path were nothing more than faint and constricted circles of light. Far off, a fog-horn sounded its plaintive call, and against that distant sound their footsteps were unnaturally loud on the gravel.

'I like this,' Lucas observed when they reached the dark path through the trees. He paused, releasing her hand to stretch, flexing his shoulders, rising up on his toes, then back on his heels...and all the while Jenny watched, absorbing the lines and the whipcord strength of that powerful body. 'This is good,' he announced, standing motionless, listening to the hushed silence and the counterpoint of the fog-horn's call. 'Peaceful, isn't it?'

'Magic,' Jenny agreed, speaking as softly as he had. 'There's something about fog... It makes the world go away, makes anything possible.'

'More of that romantic streak of yours?' he quizzed, taking her hand again, leading her towards the end of the tunnel made by the trees. At the edge of the lawn they stopped by a hedge of wild roses and started up to where the inn should have been but no longer was. 'Either the fog's very thick or they moved the place while we were gone.'

'I know what happened. It floated away,' she decided, her voice dreamy. 'While we were gone, it just floated away. Now it's miles away, somewhere out at sea, and we missed being rocked to sleep by the waves.'

'Spoken like a true romantic,' he told her, sounding amused, and then the amusement disappeared, replaced by a deeper, seductively teasing note. 'You *are* a romantic, aren't you, Jennifer?'

'I——' She hesitated, then abandoned caution to the winds. She couldn't lie to him, not here in the misty darkness, the scent of roses heavy in the air. Besides, there was something tempting in the way his fingers were stroking her palm; it was an intensely exciting and intimate gesture, one which had already reduced her to a state beyond pretence. 'More than most people know.'

'Because you keep it so well hidden. It's something you're afraid to admit—I wonder why—so you keep it hidden away.' He took one step forward, still holding her hand, then stopped and turned her to face him. 'But not from me.' His lips touched hers briefly—once, twice, then again and again, playing a game with her senses.

CHAPTER FOUR

SUDDENLY—in an instant, Jenny realised—it stopped being a game. Lucas carried her hand to his chest and spread it, palm down, over the increasing beat of his heart. They were alone in the hushed and misty night, and she didn't try to analyse the current between them when he drew her into his arms and moulded her into the hard length of him. All she knew—all she needed to know—was that she wanted him, and that—incredibly!—he wanted her too. Her lips willingly parted to the increasing pressure of his. His hunger and her answering need were a palpable force; beneath her hand, his heartbeat was racing now, in time with her own.

This was real, she acknowledged. This was better and deeper and stronger—more than she could ever have imagined. The realisation rocked her, left her feeling giddy and weak with longing. Her free hand went to his shoulder in an ineffectual attempt to steady herself, then stayed to savour the hard-corded muscles, the power and grace of this man.

'Jennifer, Jennifer...' He covered her face with kisses, his fingers tangling in her hair while his lips trailed fire along her throat and the curve of her shoulder. 'Do you have any idea what you're doing to me?'

She nodded, feeling it in the tumbling beat of his heart, in the muscles knotting beneath her touch, hearing it in his strained breathing. She knew as well what he was doing to her: creating magic, something she hadn't known existed, an incredible piercing sweetness in her.

'And what you're doing to me...' she attempted shyly '...well, it's lovely.'

'It's all more than that,' he told her, a deeper note in his voice, his lips like fire on her skin, 'and I don't want it to end.'

Neither did she, she realised, but to acknowledge the feeling was to destroy the wild excitement growing within her. This was madness, she knew, suddenly stiff and unresponsive in his embrace. She was already in deeper than she had ever been with Ralph; she was perilously close to crossing a line she'd never come close to with any man. She was a fool! In spite of this evening, she still knew almost nothing about Lucas; to give him this kind of power over her was insane. 'Lucas—please——' she began, wondering how to explain, afraid that she'd left it too long.

But he was miles ahead of her—more objective, she guessed, more aware of each shading between them. 'What's the trouble, Jenny?' he asked, lifting his head, his hands light on her shoulders as he stared down at her. 'Don't you trust me?'

Of course not! she thought, wishing she could—but he was a man, wasn't he? Except for her father, she'd never known a man she could trust. There was nothing— nothing yet!—about Lucas to make her believe she could trust him...any more than she should have trusted Ralph.

'Jenny, I'm nothing at all like that man.'

'Perhaps not,' she conceded evenly, forcing herself to hide the confusion his words had created. He'd read her mind with uncanny accuracy—was this a sign that she could trust him, or was he simply too clever for her? 'Still, you're rushing me, Lucas.' She turned slightly, slipping away from his touch.

'You're probably right,' he agreed with an odd, twisted smile. 'We need time—time for you to get used to the idea of me, and time for me to convince you that you can trust me. Jenny——' Without warning, he caught her to him again, kissed her again—a slow, lingering kiss—then released her, all but her hand. 'Jenny, this is *real*,' he told her, his expression suddenly solemn. 'I already know that I want you, and I'll wait however long it takes you to believe that my intentions—as the old saying goes—are strictly honourable.'

Something was nagging at her, something soft but insistent. Restlessly, Jenny turned and pulled the sheet over her head, trying to shut out that niggling sound and the light. The light? Lord, it couldn't be light yet—could it? Experimentally, she opened one eye, instantly more awake when she saw bright sunlight pouring into her room, heard the soft tapping at her door.

'Jenny? Jenny, are you awake? Are you there?'

Tessa, Jenny registered, but only barely, groaning as she threw off the sheet and got out of bed. She hadn't had nearly enough sleep, she thought resentfully. It felt like only a very few hours, which was probably right, and what she got for lying awake half the night. She'd come back to her room in a fever of excitement, straining her memory to recall every detail of her magic evening with Lucas, every nuance of the kiss they had shared, savouring what he had said at the end.

His intentions! What a wealth of possibilities lay in that phrase, and Jenny had dared to play them all out. She had done something she'd thought she'd never do again, had built dream castles in the air, imagined a glowing—even dazzling—future for herself...with Lucas Lambert!

'Jenny, are you there?'

'Yes. Just a sec,' she called, pulling on her short terry robe before going to open the door.

'So there you are!' Tessa advanced into the room, her cool and languid grace flawed by an air of suppressed excitement. 'I don't believe you—sleeping in today! You're always finished with breakfast before I've pulled myself together enough to put in an appearance, and I'd have thought——' She stopped dead as the tiny dimensions of Jenny's room impinged on her consciousness. 'Lord, what are you doing in a shoe box like this?'

'Saving money, Tessa dear,' Jenny offered on a muffled yawn. 'This seemed like the year to economise.'

'Is business really that bad?' Tessa raised one eyebrow in enquiry. 'I know in your last letter you said that things had been slow, but this is ridiculous! Aren't you carrying things just a little too far?'

'Not at the moment,' Jenny countered, awake with a vengeance and suddenly grim. Then, remembering her plans to beat Ralph at his game and Lucas's agreement to purchase her car—*everything* about Lucas, in fact—she finished with glowing intensity, 'but things are about to change for the better.'

'I'd say they already had,' Tessa observed, and, even when she turned away to spread up the bed before perching on the edge, Jenny could tell that Tessa's air of excitement had returned. 'After all, you've managed to snag *the* most exciting and impossibly sexy man ever to attend this or any other antique car meet. At least, I assume you managed to snag him,' she continued, fixing Jenny with her most appraising look. 'How else to explain why neither one of you made an appearance at last night's festivities?'

'We had dinner,' Jenny explained, smiling at the memories of that wonderful evening, 'and we talked for a while.'

'Only talked?' Tessa eyed her sceptically. 'Now that I know for sure who that gorgeous man really is, I doubt that. I suppose he's the worst sort of playboy, but I think you should go for it. It's high time that you had a fling for yourself, and it must be great fun to be wined and dined—and romanced, I assume—by someone who usually only bothers with countesses and minor princesses, but——'

'What are you talking about?' Jenny demanded.

'But surely you know! I was almost positive last evening when you introduced me to him. I was going to say something, and then I decided not to. I mean, if I'd been wrong, it would have been embarrassing, wouldn't it?'

'If you'd been wrong about what?' Jenny asked with sudden foreboding, afraid that the beautiful world she'd been constructing was about to be shattered. 'Are you trying to tell me something about Lucas?'

'Of course. Lord, you don't know, do you?' Tessa went suddenly serious, almost solemn, eyeing Jenny with a slightly worried expression. 'But why on earth didn't he tell you? How did he manage... and how could you spend a whole evening with him and not realise?

'Jenny, your Lucas Lambert——' giving it her best midwestern flat pronunciation '—is none other than Luc Lambert.' This time, the name sounded completely different, Tessa's flawless French accent gilding the name with a Continental flair. 'You know,' she added in the face of Jenny's blank expression, 'the race driver—Grand Prix circuit, most successful driver ever from the US, second-best driver in the world two years running—I was given those details last night—darling of café society all over Europe... *That* sort of thing!'

'You're not serious! Are you?'

'Afraid so.' Tessa watched sympathetically as Jenny turned away to stare out of the window. 'It was all over the dining-room last night, although people could hardly believe it. I mean, what would Luc Lambert be doing *here*, at a nothing special antique car meet in Maine? But his brother-in-law—Wes something-or-other—finally confirmed it.'

'I don't believe it!' Jenny turned back from the window, eyes sparking anger. 'That bastard!'

'Who? Wes? Actually, he seemed——'

'No, not Wes,' Jenny snapped. 'Lucas...Luc—whatever he chooses to call himself. Do you know what he told me?' she demanded rhetorically. 'He said he'd been knocking around Europe, having one of the longest delayed adolescences on record.'

'Well, that's more or less true, I suppose,' Tessa offered thoughtfully, 'unless one takes auto racing seriously, which I personally don't. Perhaps he doesn't either, although I expect he'd still be doing it if he hadn't had that terrible accident a couple of years ago.'

'That accident,' Jenny echoed, rage building within her. 'He told me about that—at least he mentioned it—but he never said how... He *lied* to me!'

'Or avoided the truth,' Tessa suggested objectively, 'although I don't quite see why.'

'So he could amuse himself at my expense!' Jenny took a step, needing to pace, and found that the room was too small. Instead, she returned to the window to stare blankly out at the morning. It was all coming clear now, the things she shouldn't have missed...

It wasn't as though she knew much about Luc Lambert; she certainly didn't follow Grand Prix racing or the scandalous doings of European high society, but only someone both blind and deaf could have missed hearing about him or seeing his picture in countless newspapers and magazines or on TV.

Lucas—Luc!—was famous, the young American who had gone to Europe, using France as a base while he'd pursued his increasingly successful racing career. After ten years, he'd almost become a Frenchman, but everyone knew that he was really an American—the most successful American Grand Prix driver ever.

Everyone knew...but Jenny had missed it completely—mostly, she supposed, because like everyone else she hadn't expected someone like Luc Lambert to turn up at an antique car meet on the coast of Maine. Besides, the man she'd met yesterday, while he *was* incredibly attractive, bore very little resemblance to the Grand Prix driver she'd seen in fuzzy newspaper photos or in brief clips on TV. *That* man had been much younger, with an unlined face and boyish grin; somehow he hadn't seemed quite so tall, so mature.

But it was the same man; there was no doubt about it. The Lucas Lambert she'd thought she knew was really Luc Lambert, and she'd been mad to have been imagining a future with him. How could there be any future for her when his past was littered with all those countesses and minor princesses Tessa had mentioned, plus gorgeous movie stars and a few beautiful young women married and then divorced from incredibly rich older men? From what even Jenny had read, he'd had all those to choose from—and she'd been fool enough to think he found *her* attractive!

'Lord, I've been such a fool.' Jenny turned away from the window, distractedly running her fingers through her curls. 'I've been a hundred and one kinds of fool!'

'I don't see quite how,' Tessa ventured carefully. 'I mean, what's the harm if someone like Luc Lambert wants to spend time with you, if he finds you attractive——?'

'Ha! How can someone like that find someone like me attractive?' Jenny demanded bitterly. 'I'm nothing but a little brown wren, a country bumpkin from upstate New York. I'm not a bit like the women he finds attractive, but he told me I was, and I believed him...and he let me think he knew nothing at all about cars,' she continued, her rage building momentum. 'He just stood there and let me explain all about my car when it's his job to drive some of the most sophisticated ones in the world. I've been making fun of him for how little he knows!'

'Oh, dear,' Tessa began, then started to laugh. 'Well, perhaps he found it charming—to be treated like a normal person, not like some kind of a god or a ticket to free publicity. I'll bet you were a real novelty.'

'The kind that quickly wears off,' Jenny countered sharply, her hands clenched into fists, nails biting into her palms. When she thought of what he'd done, what he'd made her believe, she wasn't sure whether to scream or to cry. He'd fed her such an incredible line—all day long, and then last night... No, last night didn't bear thinking about!

'This is *real*,' he'd told her, when he'd known there was nothing real about it! All the time, the whole thing had been a fake, a series of lies... 'He's only been playing with me,' she said now, her voice ragged, unsteady, 'and all the time I was believing him, all those nice things he said...'

'He may have meant them.'

'No, he was laughing at me,' Jenny said sharply, her anger building again. 'He was having fun watching me swallow his line!' He had betrayed her. Against her best instincts, she'd decided to trust him—which showed just how big a fool she was. Now, thinking about what he'd done, she was dimly aware that only the mobilising force of her rage was keeping away the pain and sense of humiliation which had briefly threatened. 'Hell,' she exploded, 'I could *kill* him!'

'You can't,' Tessa contradicted with the hint of a smile. 'He wouldn't die. The man's a survivor; anyone can see that. Besides, you're too nice a person to go around murdering people.'

'Not any more! Not about him,' Jenny snapped. Something inside her had been shattered, broken beyond repair, but she would put it behind her, just as she had once before. 'I know I can't kill him, but the least I can do from now on is cut him dead—*very* dead!'

For the next couple of hours, Jenny knew, cutting Lucas dead would be a snap. Or was he Luc? she wondered wildly as she took her place on the panel at the technical session, realising that she no longer knew *what* to call him, although 'skunk' now seemed to fit better than either variation of his name. Whatever his name, she managed to avoid any eye contact for quite a while.

He was at the technical session, of course, just as she'd expected, but now that the word was out about him he was surrounded by a fawning bunch of admirers. Standing near the back of the room, he was the centre of attention, and it wasn't until the technical chairman firmly called the session to order that Lucas was able to sit down. He settled into a chair in the back row, lounging at his ease, long legs stretched out into the aisle and one arm notched over the back of his chair. Then, with the session finally underway, he looked at Jenny and smiled—that slow and easy smile she had found devastatingly intimate only the day before—and raised one hand in a brief salute.

First chance to cut him dead, she told herself, bending her head as though to study the few notes she had with her. In truth, she was finding this business of ignoring him more difficult than she'd expected. She might hate him for what he'd been doing to her, but that didn't change the fact that he was an attractive man and that she'd been—still was, she admitted reluctantly—attracted to him.

Yes, but forget about that! she lectured herself, doggedly working her way through all she knew about engine running temperatures and their effects on spark plugs and oil. It was dull stuff, but Lucas—Luc!—followed the discussion more closely than she might have liked. Each time she glanced in his direction, he was watching her with the same intensity and appreciation that had left her breathless the previous day. It threatened to leave her just as breathless now, and if she hadn't laboured to keep a firm grip on herself his gaze would have knocked out of her head every thought about engine temperatures. As it was, she hung on—if only barely— to her expert knowledge until the session finally ended.

Instantly, she started from the room, refusing to even look in his direction. That was easy enough to accomplish, given the tight knot of people around him, until—just as she was about to reach the door and the safety which lay beyond—the knot parted and she found herself face to face with him.

'I'm impressed,' he told her, smiling engagingly down, and before she could stop him his hand was on her arm to guide her from the room. 'Never in my wildest dreams did I expect to find a woman like you.'

'Really?' She cast him a cool, slanting glance, grateful for the protection of others around them. 'I find that hard to believe.'

'You shouldn't,' he countered easily, edging her away from the others, and, short of digging in her heels and making a scene, Jenny didn't see how she could stop him. 'I meant every word.' He increased the pressure of his grip on her arm, using his free hand to push open the door. 'I'm only telling the truth, which you'd know if you didn't have these sudden bouts of insecurity. You sat up there looking absolutely adorable while you came out with all that incredibly technical data. I was dazzled!'

'I doubt that.' She knew she ought to refuse to pass through the door, refuse to go where he was leading her, but the temptation to let him know exactly what she thought of him was too great to resist. 'You're the famous racing driver! I can't believe that you were interested in the running temperatures of antique cars,' she fumed, momentarily blinded by bright sunlight, almost stumbling on the gravel drive. 'You probably know more about the effects of running temperatures on spark plugs and oil than I ever will.'

'Ah.' He was silent for an instant. 'Is that what this is about? That you've found out what I used to do?'

'What you *are*,' she corrected, her tone aggrieved. '*Who* you are. You might have told me!'

'You're right,' he agreed, finally stopping their forward progress on the edge of the lawn where the cars were parked. He turned to face her, his hand still gripping her arm. 'I should have.'

'Then why didn't you?' she demanded, staring defiantly up at him.

'I was having too much fun.'

'I just bet you were—laughing at me, having your joke for the day!'

'It was no joke, Jennifer,' he told her, his gaze a burning silver, slowly turning her bones to water. 'It meant——' He interrupted himself, swearing fluently under his breath as someone hailed him. 'We can't talk here! Come on,' he urged, and she was marched, lockstep, across the lawn. 'We'll take your car.'

'It's yours now—remember?' she said crossly, watching as he reached into the compartment under the seat for the crank. 'Or was that just another part of your joke for the day?'

'It wasn't a joke—none of it was!—and it isn't mine until you have the cheque in your hands,' he said shortly, then paused in the act of inserting the crank to look up at her, his eyes still molten silver. 'Jenny, don't be angry, at least not until you've heard me out. Surely you owe me that much?'

She owed him nothing, she knew, but she also knew that she couldn't refuse. His will was too strong, she acknowledged, admitting defeat, and somewhere beneath her anger she'd been hoping he could explain himself. Automatically, she produced the ornate little brass key from her pocket, inserted it and then set the spark and throttle, watching as he turned and bent to the crank.

'Let's go,' he said briefly, swinging himself up beside her when the car had clattered to life.

Obediently, she shifted into first gear, and the car began to move forward. Why am I letting him do this to me? she wondered as they swept down the drive. She knew that she ought to stop the car and order him to get out, but she was already past that point. This time was different—not as it had been with Ralph. Ralph had never mattered the way Lucas already did; cutting Ralph out of her life hadn't been hard, but Lucas—well, Lucas was different. Already she was so attracted to him, so *mad* about him that she no longer had a will of her own.

It was obvious that he'd had the whole thing thought out in advance. He had told her to drive into town and park the car on the main street. He took the brass key— 'So you won't leave without me,' he told her with a heart-stopping smile—when he climbed down from his seat to buy them the makings of a picnic lunch. In due time, he returned with a bag under each arm, deposited them in the rear boot and climbed back into the car.

'Now we'll go back to yesterday's spot,' he instructed when they were under way once again. 'I can't think of a better spot for a picnic, can you?'

She couldn't think of a more *dangerous* spot than that isolated pine grove at the top of the hill, but she didn't object. She couldn't. He had her too completely under his spell now; he was too close for her to think clearly, his right arm draped casually over the back of her seat, his thigh brushing hers lightly each time they took a curve. Inside her, a wild, strange excitement was beginning to build as she thought of the two of them alone in that sun-dappled shade. She no longer cared what excuse he might give her; it would just be enough if he kissed her again...

Still, when she'd driven up the rough track and shut down the engine, she felt bound to put up some kind of resistance. 'All right, you've got what you wanted,' she said shortly, climbing down from the car, ignoring his hand, outstretched to help her. 'Now explain why you didn't tell me.'

'Because it didn't matter,' he told her, standing just before her, his gaze holding her still. 'It's not what I am, or at least not what I'd like to be.'

'Don't give me that,' she said coldly, her anger suddenly real again. 'You may be sick of being the great macho racing driver, but have you made yourself forget everything you *must* know about cars? Damn you! You made me think you knew nothing! You let me explain all those minor technical points...all those things you probably know more about than *I* do. Why didn't you stop me?'

'I couldn't help myself,' he confessed with a smile, reaching out to take both her hands, drawing her closer. 'I loved listening to you.'

'Amusing yourself at my expense,' she accused, trying to keep her anger alive. He had already released her hands to rest his at her waist, making it that much more difficult to concentrate on the injustice of what he'd done. 'You weren't being honest with me.'

'I know,' he agreed instantly, 'and that wasn't fair, but don't you see? It felt so good to be with someone who had no idea who I was, and you obviously didn't, or you wouldn't have been explaining things to me. It was grand not to have to wonder if you were attracted to me, or just to the glamour you thought there must be in what I used to do for a living.'

'I wasn't...' she attempted, but his hands were moving down from her waist to her hips, weakening her resolve, and the betraying breathlessness had returned '... attracted to you,' she finally managed.

'Liar,' he teased, drawing her even closer, until her body finally touched his. 'You were—you *are*—just as attracted to me as I am to you.'

'But it doesn't make sense,' she objected weakly, her body playing her traitor, already moulding itself into his. Then, beyond good judgement or prudence, she got to the crux of her quarrel with him. 'It must be a game to you... I can't matter! I'm nothing at all like the women you spend your time with. I'm not sophisticated or clever or——'

'And thank heaven for that. Jennifer, you're miles ahead of the women I used to spend my time with,' he told her, his voice thickening, the words coming more slowly. 'You're beautiful, incredibly so, and exciting——'

He broke off, his lips teasing at hers, destroying all her defences. She knew she shouldn't have come here with him, shouldn't be letting him do this to her, but what she knew no longer mattered. He'd won, and she tangled her fingers in his hair to draw him closer, her lips willingly parting when his mouth closed over hers to deepen their kiss.

This was what she wanted, and feminine instinct took over, compelling her to move closer still, within his embrace. It was that same instinct that helped her to understand his answering need, the taut, hard line of his body, the barely checked strength of his kiss and the way he bent her back to plunder her mouth, to trail fiery kisses down her throat.

'Jennifer, you're a witch,' he murmured, his lips moving on her skin, seeking the swell of her breast. 'Can you doubt how I feel?'

Doubt! That one word registered in her mind, and she abruptly pulled away, in a panic. Of course she could doubt him! He had lied to her—withheld the truth, anyway—given her no reason to think he was any better than Ralph. It was all too confusing, this strange mixture of doubt and desire, and she needed time. 'Can't we eat?' she asked shortly, seizing the first excuse she could think of.

'All right,' he agreed with a broad grin—knowing, she supposed, exactly how she was feeling—'if that's what you want.'

But was it? she wondered, watching him take his purchases from the boot of the car, feeling oddly bereft. Was it better to think and analyse—and have doubts— or to lose herself to the emotion, the wild excitement, the *wanting* she found in his arms? It was better not to think, she finally concluded, but it wasn't wise. It was certainly safer to keep some distance between them, and when he'd finished spreading out their picnic on the soft carpet of pine needles she took pains to maintain that distance.

CHAPTER FIVE

LUCAS had brought enough to feed an army: cold meat and cheeses, crusty rolls, salads, fresh fruit and a selection of pastries. He hadn't forgotten paper plates, napkins, plastic cutlery and glasses—even a bottle of chilled white wine.

'It's a feast,' she observed as she helped herself and he poured the wine. 'Where on earth did you find everything?'

'Up and down the main street, while you stayed by the car and fielded questions. Do people always gather around when you're out with that car?'

'Always, unless there aren't any people—like here,' she told him between bites. 'I've often thought that it must be a little like being famous, one of those people who can't go out in public without being bothered... *You're* one of those people, aren't you?' she finished, not so much a question as a statement, or even an accusation.

'I have been,' he agreed evenly, but there was an odd twist to his smile. 'But that's over now. The whole business is over now—the racing, the lifestyle——'

'The women,' she put in quickly.

'Touché,' he murmured, and had the grace to wince before he grinned. 'But I didn't spend *all* my time with them, by the way. The Press badly exaggerated my social life, along with everything else, but it was something of a merry-go-round, and I'm glad I finally had the sense to get off.'

'But why did you?' she asked, wanting, even needing, to understand him, and determined to take full advantage of his sudden candour. 'What made you decide?'

'That accident.'

'But—you're over that now, aren't you? At least, you look as though you are.'

'Oh, they patched me together reasonably well,' he allowed, 'except on the odd rainy day, when some of the patches feel stiff. No, I'm physically over the accident; it's just that running into a wall at a hundred and fifty miles an hour tends to knock some sense into a person.'

'Is *that* what you did?' she demanded, caught somewhere between awe and horror. 'You were going that fast?'

'Didn't you read all about it?' he asked with that same odd twist to his smile. 'I thought everybody had. I've been something of a freak these past two years, and I'd have thought, now that you know who I am, you'd know all the gory details. Everyone else seems to.'

'Sorry, but I don't,' she said crisply, then tried to think back. 'I suppose I was vaguely aware of the accident, but I don't get my fun reading about gory details. And I am *not* like everyone else!'

'I know that,' he admitted, relaxing slightly, giving her a real smile this time. 'In fact, I seem to spend an inordinate amount of my time trying to convince you that part of your attraction is just that.

'And yes,' he continued after a moment, beginning to build an enormous sandwich, 'I did run into a wall at that speed—something I don't recommend, although it is an extraordinarily effective way to clarify thinking...that plus many months in various hospitals, wired together and held in place by weights and pulleys. It gave me plenty of time to consider whether or not I liked the way my life was going.'

'And you decided you didn't like racing,' Jenny supplied.

He nodded, biting into his sandwich and chewing reflectively before going on. 'It's an incredibly lonely life, unless all you care about is the driving. I was travelling most of the year, no time to put down any roots, no chance to get hold of anything solid. You wondered how I managed to find all this——' his free hand gestured, indicating their feast '—but that's one of my few real talents. I've learned how to go into any strange town and find almost anything I want. Instant...not home, precisely, but instant tolerable living conditions.'

'Instant roots?' Jenny suggested.

He shook his head. 'No. No roots at all, and that was the problem. There comes a time when a man is too old to keep playing the gypsy...and I also began to dislike the choices.'

'What choices?'

'The difficult ones,' he said after another bite of his sandwich. 'The kind of driving I did is full of difficult choices, but the worst was almost two years ago when I had to decide whether to crash into a friend who'd spun out just ahead, or take a cement wall at speed. The friend was married, and he and his wife had a child...'

'He had roots,' Jenny said softly.

He nodded, staring hard at his sandwich. 'And...in the relative scheme of things, it seemed that I was considerably more expendable than he was, so I chose the wall.'

There had been no calculation in that decision, she knew without any doubt. When he dealt with her, there was always room for doubt and distrust, but she knew that what he'd just told her was very real. Given a choice between the possibility of his friend's death or his own, Lucas had instinctively made the decision to sacrifice himself.

That, she realised, was the kind of friend Lucas was, the kind of friend he'd been to her the previous evening when he'd heard her out about Ralph and offered to loan her the money she needed. Beneath Luc Lambert was the Lucas Lambert for whom friendship was an absolute, for whom loyalty and sincerity were inviolate. And just my luck that I bring out so much of the *Luc* in him, she thought resentfully, almost wistfully. Why can't I be just a *friend*?

'So—what about you?' he asked, his voice so unexpected in the sun-dappled silence that she jumped, spilling a little of her wine on her hand.

'About me?' she asked, bending her head to touch her tongue to the wine on her hand. 'What about me?' She lifted her head and then froze when she saw the way he was looking at her, the way he was smiling—heavy-lidded, knowing and intimate. As though he can see what I'm thinking, Jenny told herself. He knows, and he wants me to know that we can't be friends. He wants more—or less—than friendship. He won't let me get out of this as easily, as safely, as that. Just then he reached out his hand, and she pulled back, instinctively trying to avoid his touch.

But all he did was pick up an apple from the pile of fruit between them. He studied it for a moment, then absently rubbed it on his shirt. 'What's made you the person you are?' he finally asked, then bit into the apple with strong white teeth, chewing with obvious pleasure before continuing, 'You're not exactly doing what one expects of a pretty girl.' He paused for another bite of the apple. 'You could get by just standing around and being decorative, and restoring antique cars is usually considered to be a man's job. Why did you go into it? To please your father?'

'No, although it did please him, of course,' Jenny answered readily, grateful to be given something safe to talk about. Now, if she could just stop herself from watching—absorbing!—Lucas as he ate that apple, the indolent grace of his movements, the breadth of his shoulders, the length of his legs . . . 'No, it was just what I wanted to do. I'd always been around the cars, always spent a lot of time with Dad at the shop.'

'And your mother?'

'Didn't approve, of course. The last thing she wanted was for me to be a tomboy, but nothing she said or did could stop me.' Jenny leaned forward again, forgetting herself in the past. 'I loved everything to do with the cars. I loved helping Dad on them, and thinking about what they'd been and could become again. They'd come in unrestored, some in terrible shape. One I remember had been used as a chicken coop, and another still had a bees' nest in the back seat—complete with bees. When they were that bad, I'd think about what they'd been through in all the years since they were new. Then, after Dad had restored them, they'd be new again. It didn't matter if it was a Model T Ford or a Rolls-Royce—any restored car could give me a glimpse of a world in the past, and I loved that,' she finished, staring down at her glass.

'Like yesterday afternoon, when you brought me here. You called it a different world . . . and romantic,' he reminded her, and she could hear the smile in his voice.

'Yes, I said that,' she acknowledged reluctantly, abruptly recalled to the reality of what Lucas—*Luc*—had been doing to her. For a little while there he'd swept her away, made her forget that he was a smooth operator from an alien world, that he'd played a shabby trick on her by not telling her from the start who he really was. 'But I shouldn't have said that to *you*!'

'Why not?'

Why not? Because I didn't want to put ideas in your head, because I would rather have been your friend than your little romance for the weekend. 'Because it was a stupid thing to say to someone like you,' she finally managed, drawing her knees up, leaning her head against them so she wouldn't have to face him. 'You're so—so worldly. And I'm not.'

'Thank heaven for that.' His voice, deep and intimate, sounded close to her ear, as though he'd drawn nearer, to bend his head towards hers. 'I don't want worldly, Jennifer. I want you. I knew it almost the moment I saw you.' She felt his hand on her shoulder, his fingers stroking the skin that was instantly sensitive and alive to his touch. 'Jennifer, look at me,' he commanded, and when she didn't comply his hand moved to her cheek, compelling her to face him again. 'Jenny, you're special.'

'No, I'm not!' No one knew that better than she did, yet there was no denying the warmth of his smile, or the lazy spark kindling in his eyes.

'You're wrong. I watched you move with such grace, such pride of ownership each time you touched your car. And then, when you offered me a ride, when you pulled out the crank and started it up, it was an incredible feeling for me.' Briefly, he kissed her, his lips warm against hers. 'I knew then, even if I hadn't before, that you were——'

'Odd,' she supplied unsteadily.

'No. Unique.' He kissed her again, his lips lingering this time, coaxing until she began to respond. 'That's right,' he told her, withdrawing slightly, his hands tracing the delicate bones of her shoulders. 'You're so fragile,' he breathed, 'so fragile to touch, and I want to touch every inch...'

In spite of her doubts, she wanted that too, Jenny acknowledged, suddenly dizzy with longing. It was madness; she knew it was madness, this attraction between them. For him it meant nothing, but if she gave in to him now she'd be badly hurt—a pain far greater than the pain Ralph had inflicted. Remember that! she urged herself fiercely as Lucas leaned closer and murmured her name.

'No...please don't,' she whispered, shaking her head, placing her hands on his chest to push him away—a mistake, she realised instantly. His thin knit shirt was no real barrier to her touch; she could feel the heat of his body against her palms. With a will of their own, her fingers spread, to savour that heat and his hard-muscled strength.

'That's right,' he said, drawing her closer, his touch intensely exciting—like fire, she thought—as his caresses grew bolder. 'Jenny, darling, don't make me stop.'

'I don't think I can,' she admitted, as instinct betrayed her. Something new was stirring within her, something wild coming to life, compelling her to respond.

'Jenny...my love,' he murmured, his lips teasing hers in brief, tempting kisses, turning to lay her back on the soft carpet of pine needles, the weight of his body poised just over hers. 'Jennifer, I want to make love to you.'

She wanted that too, she acknowledged, reaching up to him, her hands tracing the contours of his hard flesh. But still, it wasn't enough, she realised vaguely. She needed more, needed the weight of his body on hers...needed all of him to satisfy the unbearable tension he'd created in her. 'Lucas, please,' she said on a sigh, linking her arms around his neck, the incredible magic of his touch driving her, forcing her to draw him closer.

'Ah, Jennifer...' his voice was rough and unsteady '...my love...Jenny, does anyone ever come here?' he asked urgently.

'No,' she told him, beyond any pretence now, her fingers tangling in his crisp hair. 'No one,' she promised. Then, realising the magnitude—the consequences—of

what she'd just told him, she struggled to gather the tat-
tered remnants of her resolve. 'But we——'

'No, no buts, Jennifer.'

She should stop him; she knew she should, but how
could she? His touch was magic, too powerful to resist.
Gently, he caressed the swell of her breast, then she heard
her own small gasp of mingled shock and excitement
when he slipped both his hands beneath her T-shirt. His
fingers traced unbelievably intricate patterns on her skin
and she said his name, arching towards him, trying to
finish the unbearable game he was playing.

Her surrender complete now, she slipped over the edge
into the new and incredible world he had created. She
kneaded his shoulders, drew her hands along the hard
planes of his chest, heard his own ragged gasp mingle
with hers when his hand finally closed over her breast.

'Jenny, I need you,' he breathed as he bent his head
to her breast, piercing her with the gentle torment of his
tongue.

Now it was all sensation: his hands and his lips on her
skin, the taste of salt on her tongue when she kissed the
base of his throat. She was on fire, wild with desire,
wanting more. Mindlessly, her fingers tangled again in
his hair to hold him close and closer still... Then, in
the far distance, she heard the laughter of a child, felt
Lucas stiffen against her. *No!* she thought in the same
moment she heard him swear under his breath. 'Someone's coming,' she whispered, feeling sick.

'Damn right,' he agreed grimly, abruptly drawing
away, his hands not quite steady when he pulled her shirt
back into place. 'And you said no one comes here,' he
accused, his tone gentling.

'But no one does,' she wailed, scrambling into a sitting
position. 'At least I've never seen anyone.'

'An incredible piece of timing.' He smiled, a tight and
twisted smile, then with brief economy plucked some

pine needles from her hair. 'You look tousled,' he added with another, easier smile. 'Your mother wouldn't approve.'

'She wouldn't believe it,' Jenny contributed in her own attempt at humour—anything to help her deal with the terrible awkwardness of the moment. 'I'm not sure *I* do!'

'Well, you'd better,' he told her, grim again. 'Jenny——'

'Daddy, look at this car!' they heard a young voice exclaim, much closer this time. 'It's weird!'

'It's an antique, Gil,' an older male voice replied, 'from the meet down at the inn. Careful, don't touch it. We'll see if we can find the owner and ask him about it.'

'You're the owner now, Lucas,' Jenny reminded him, regaining some of her poise. 'It's your job now to tell them about it.'

In the end, though, they were both drawn into the lengthy question and answer session which followed. It was some time before they were done and the boy and his father, out for a day's hiking in the woods, went on their way.

When they had, Lucas turned to Jenny, his expression grave. 'We were lucky, you know,' he said quietly. 'If they hadn't come along... Do you realise how close we came?'

'I——' She swallowed painfully. She didn't need Lucas to tell her how close they had come. She knew, and she cursed herself for the revealing colour she knew was staining her face. They'd been completely out of control—*she'd* been completely out of control, she amended. She doubted that he had. He'd probably known exactly what he was doing the whole time. After all, this kind of experience must have happened to him hundreds of times, while for her... Well, she'd never felt anything like it before, never responded, never *wanted*... It didn't bear thinking about, but she had to face facts. She had to remember just how clever Lucas could be, how easily he could destroy all her defences... 'It must never happen again,' she said in a tight, hurried voice.

'Not like that, anyway,' he agreed, sounding grim. 'If we hadn't been interrupted——' He paused, drawing a deep breath. 'I didn't intend—I should have stopped... It happened too soon, not the way I want it to be. Believe it or not, Jennifer Howe, I want something more than a roll in the hay with you.'

'Oh! Please——' She turned away, feeling a little sick. 'Please don't call it that.'

She heard him sigh, then his arms were around her waist, drawing her rigid form back against him. 'Jenny...Jennifer, what has happened between us is more than that, and we're going to keep it that way. What I want,' he continued, his voice a persuasive, seductive murmur just above her ear, 'is something better and deeper... I want a proper, old-fashioned courtship.'

A courtship! Did he mean it? she asked herself, her heart leaping, catching in her throat. That phrase, if he really meant it, made all the difference. If it wasn't just fun he was after, if she meant more to him than a weekend's amusement, then surely that made what had happened between them all right.

A courtship, she thought, repeating, savouring that old-fashioned phrase. If he meant it... but of course he did! He must! How could she not believe the conviction in his voice? She had to believe that he meant what he said; she *had* to trust him! After all, he was already her world—her sun, moon and stars.

'Better now?' he asked softly when he felt the tension leaving her body. 'You believe me?'

'Yes,' she promised, and felt his lips, feather-light on her forehead.

'Good. Then let's go back and get ready for that awards banquet they've laid on for tonight.' He hesitated briefly, then turned her to face him. 'You'll have to meet Carole and Wes, I'm afraid,' he told her, choosing his words, she thought, with particular care. 'There's no way we can avoid them...but meeting my family surely qualifies as proper courtship activity. You should know, though, that they're everything I'm not...and have nothing I want.'

Because of that cryptic comment, Jenny hadn't been sure what to expect, but as soon as she met Carole and Wes she fervently hoped that Lucas had meant what he'd said. Wes wasn't so bad, she supposed. He was a middle-aged businessman who was just a little too smooth, too unctuous, for her to feel completely comfortable in his presence. But Carole—well, Carole was something else!

'So this is the girl who's been taking up all your time,' Carole commented with a silvery laugh which rang slightly false to Jenny's ears. Carole's busy gaze studied Jenny's appearance with an expert's shrewd calculation.

Before she had left her room, Jenny had thought she looked good. It was true that her dress hadn't cost much, but she had liked its pale pink colour and flowing lines, had thought that it went well with her cloud of dark curls. Now Carole, in an instant, had made her feel shabby and second-rate, that her dress was too garish and her hair too untamed.

Carole, by contrast, was perfect, intimidatingly perfect. Her face was flawless, and not an ash-blonde hair was out of place, its apparent disorder deliberate and artfully contrived. Carole's outfit was surely by a top designer: a dress and jacket of bias-cut silk, jade-green, hot orange and cool white. Her jewellery was of jade and diamonds, substantial pieces to perfectly complement her clothes, the whole effect an example of wonderful taste and the means to display it.

There was money here—serious money, Jenny realised. She was sitting tonight with people like Ralph's fat cat, and he was welcome to them! She didn't like the type, and she hated being made to feel like one of the hired help.

'How clever of you, to know all about cars,' Carole observed with another of her silvery laughs, making it clear that she considered Jenny not so much clever as odd. 'I'm very stupid about them, and I couldn't bear messing about with them and getting dirty.'

'That's why soap was invented,' Lucas said, his words clipped and cold, and Carole's lips pursed in displeasure. She turned away, leaving it to her husband to attempt to maintain the conversational thread of civility.

'Of course, Luc's always been mad about cars,' Wes offered smoothly, 'which is why it's so lucky that he stumbled on to you. He's a bit at sixes and sevens right now,' he continued directly to Jenny. 'He claims to have given up his racing career——'

'I *have* given it up,' Lucas interjected firmly, but Wes ignored him.

'—which is why he needs something to occupy his time, until he changes his mind.'

'But he shouldn't!' Carole re-entered the conversation now. 'It would be better—safer, too—to have some sort of suitable hobby, and antique cars would seem ideal. Lucas, I don't see why you don't just buy that one——'

'Well, nothing's definite yet,' Wes broke in to say. 'It's not a sure thing.'

'And it was never *my* idea,' Lucas reminded them both.

'Besides,' Jenny heard herself saying, determined to get a word in, 'he's already agreed to buy mine.'

'Isn't that nice?' Wes was all hearty charm. 'That's a fine little car.'

'You know it?' Jenny asked, surprised.

'Oh, yes. I've been eyeing that little beauty as much as Luc's been eyeing you.' The idea seemed to amuse him.

It would, Jenny thought distastefully, suspecting that Wes himself wasn't averse to eyeing the occasional woman. He was an obvious type, while Carole was more subtle, and Jenny could find nothing to like in either of them. Still, their presence couldn't spoil her evening, any more than Ralph's could.

He was sitting only two tables away. Occasionally, throughout the meal, she'd felt his gaze on her, and the once or twice she'd looked in his direction she'd seen him glowering at her. Poor Ralph, she thought, feeling deliciously smug. She was sitting with some of those fat cats whose company he coveted. Even worse, from his point of view, must be his growing suspicion that she was selling her car to someone other than his own fat cat. Surely he was beginning to realise that he'd lost the game. How he must hate her! she told herself with a small glow of triumph. He'd spent two years planning her downfall, and now it was all turning to ashes for him.

And all thanks to Lucas, she mused, instinctively turning to reassure herself of his presence beside her. He had to be the most attractive man in the room; surely everyone was as awed as she was by the way his dinner-jacket lay on his broad shoulders, and by the contrast between its white purity and the depth of his tan! Lucas was, quite simply, a splendid man, and he'd made an incredibly splendid difference in her life.

It would have been enough if all he'd done was agree to buy her car. It was a wonderful feeling to know that she'd sold it so quickly and easily, without having to

swallow her pride and give Ralph the satisfaction of being
the one to arrange the sale. To go begging to Ralph would
have killed her, and briefly the injustice of what he'd
attempted to do burned fierce within her.

The nerve of the man! The absolute, incredible gall!
After what he'd done to ruin her business, he'd actually
thought he could profit from her one attempt to correct
the damage he'd done. Lord, what a devious and almost
perfect scheme it had been, to earn—what? Possibly ten
or twenty per cent of the sale price of her car as a finder's
fee when the only reason she was selling it was because
of what *he* had done to her!

But Lucas had rescued her from that final humiliation. He was buying her car, no questions asked... Yes,
that would have been enough, but there was so much
more to Lucas than that. There was his charm and attraction, and—after that silly misunderstanding about
his not telling her who he really was—there was such
rapport between them, such a closeness. And there was
even more than that, she reminded herself, suddenly
feeling warm and protected, as though she'd come home
after years of wandering. He'd said it, hadn't he? He'd
told her that he liked her as she was, that she was sexy,
exciting, a witch, that he wanted her... That he wanted
a proper, old-fashioned courtship, and that could mean
only one thing! A courtship led to a marriage, she mused,
savouring the idea of spending the rest of her life with
this incredible, wonderful man.

It was a final touch, the icing on her particular cake,
to win the Best in Show award. She had been so absorbed by Lucas all weekend that she hadn't given the
matter a thought, so she was listening with only half an
ear when the meet chairman reached the final award of
the evening.

'And now, what you've all been waiting for,' he in-
toned into the microphone, continuing with some plati-

tudes about how many fine cars there had been to choose from, how hard the judging had been. 'And it was even more difficult this year,' he explained, 'because the car many of the judges thought might be the best was so seldom around to be judged. But they finally got the chance, just before the banquet started, and now it's official—this year's winner of Best in Show is one of our own—Sam Howe's daughter Jenny's 1904 Franklin Runabout! Jenny, come up to receive your award!'

'Oh!' When she heard her name, Jenny felt as though all the breath had been knocked out of her. She had never won a Best in Show before, hadn't given it a thought this time, wasn't sure just how to react. Then, gathering her scattered wits, she stood, then abruptly sat down again. 'Lucas, shouldn't you go?' she appealed under the cover of the applause. 'After all, it's your car now.'

'Not on your life,' he told her with a comforting squeeze of her hand. 'It's still yours—remember? You don't have my cheque yet, so do as the man said—go collect your prize,' he ordered, and filled her cup to overflowing when he soundly kissed her.

Just like that! she mused as she floated towards the meet chairman. Lucas had kissed her in front of everyone, in front of Carole and Wes—and how Carole, especially, must have hated that! Had ever a night been so grand, so perfect, as this one?

The heavy brass and hardwood trophy was placed in her hands, she spoke a few words of thanks into the microphone, then started back to Lucas, wanting nothing so much as to be with him again. But people kept getting in her way, slowing her progress, stopping her to offer their congratulations.

Bother...such a bore, she thought more than once, clutching her award, making distracted, monosyllabic responses to the things people were saying to her. There was a time when a Best in Show award would have mattered terribly to her, but that time had passed. What was a Best in Show award when she had Lucas?

And where was he? she wondered when she finally caught sight of their table, now empty. Where had he gone? she asked herself, fighting a sudden and irrational sense of panic. All her old insecurities, all her old doubts and fears came rushing back, until she finally caught sight of him, taller than anyone else. He was standing in a quiet corner, his back to her, talking to someone hidden by his large form.

Lucas, she called silently, working a few steps closer before she was stopped again. Then, blessedly, a clear path to him opened up for her, and she was nearly upon him before she was hailed again.

Honestly! Not someone else, she thought, impatient, backing away from the man even as he spoke to her. 'Yes…perhaps another time,' she promised him, smiling apologetically, closing the distance to Lucas, until she was only a step or two away. 'I'll talk to you in the morning,' she added rashly to the stranger, turning towards the impressive breadth of Lucas's shoulders.

'…got the car, didn't you?' she heard someone saying, a voice sounding uncannily like Ralph's. 'You got what you wanted.'

'I did,' that was Lucas, cold and clipped, using a tone Jenny had never heard him use before, 'but no thanks to you.'

'What are you talking about?' the man talking to Lucas demanded angrily, and Jenny shivered. It *was* Ralph's voice, she realised. It was Ralph, and he was talking to Lucas, saying terrible things, things she wished she didn't have to hear. 'I'd say it was *all* thanks to me. I told you about it, laid the groundwork so the car *would* be for sale. That was our deal, and I pulled it off—you'd never have gotten it without me, so don't think you can back out now.'

'Don't worry, Porter, you'll get your finder's fee,' Lucas said clearly—*too* clearly, piercing Jenny's heart. 'Just stay away from me—understand?'

'Sure I do,' Ralph agreed with heavy humour, both men oblivious to Jenny, standing stricken, just behind them. 'If she finds out what I've done for you, it could ruin your little game, couldn't it? Keep her in the dark, and you can have your little fling with her.'

'But it's too late for that,' Jenny announced, finding the courage to cut between the two men, finding the courage to confront them both. 'If you wanted to discuss your little business deal, you should have waited until I wasn't around,' she told them, driven by a hot flame of rage unlike anything she'd ever known before. 'As it is, you've just lost your chance for your little fling—*and* the car!' She glared up at Lucas, her chin at a stubborn angle. 'The deal's off. My car is not for sale—not to *you*!'

She turned then, head still held high, brushing past anyone who got in her way as she made for the dining-room door, then across the lobby with its thinning crowds, towards the stairs. She had already gained the first step when she finally heard Lucas, close behind her.

'Jenny, wait,' he commanded, and she felt his hand close on her wrist. 'Let me explain.'

'What? Again?' she demanded, turning on him. 'That will make the second time today that you've had to try to explain away your lies and evasions, and I'm not such a fool that I'll fall for your line twice in one day. I should have trusted my instincts the first time, and you can be absolutely sure that I'm going to trust them now!'

'No, you're going to listen to me,' he said doggedly, his face pale beneath his tan. 'Just hear me out.'

'I won't! I don't want to hear anything you've got to say. And let me go,' she stormed.

'Not until you've listened to me. Come on, Jenny. We're attracting an audience here. Let's go outside.'

'I won't,' she said again, too angry to care about making a scene, ignoring the people beginning to gather in a circle around where she and Lucas stood. 'I'm not going anywhere with you!'

'Oh, yes, you are,' he said calmly enough, but the promise—the threat—in his tone was implicit. 'So help me, Jenny, you're coming with me—even if I have to pick you up and carry you.'

He would, too. She would put nothing past him at this point, and, while her rage was burning just as bright, she had already discovered that there were limits to how much of a scene she was prepared to make. Standing here, storming at him, was one thing—she didn't care who heard her tell him off—but her mind balked at the indignity of being bundled into his arms like a disobedient child.

Damn him! she cursed as she took the step down, watched the crowd part to permit them to pass. Damn him to hell! She had no choice but to go with him, but nothing he could say—nothing at all!—was going to change how she felt. She had let him sweet-talk her once, but that wouldn't happen again. This time was going to be different!

'This won't do any good, you know,' she told him, digging in her heels briefly, one last gesture of defiance. 'You can't play your tricks again.'

'We'll see,' he said grimly, then managed one of his patented smiles for the people watching. 'Don't mind us,' he said to them, oozing charm. 'We're just having a small lovers' quarrel, and it's time to patch things up.'

CHAPTER SIX

'LOVERS' quarrel? Don't make me laugh!' Jenny exploded, but she'd waited until they were outside. 'This is *not* a lovers' quarrel, and don't think you can patch it up. There's *no way* you can patch this one up!'

'Perhaps not, but at least you can hear me out,' Lucas said grimly, leading her further away from the inn, neither stopping nor saying anything more until they'd reached a far and shadowy corner of the garden. 'Jenny, you've got to listen to me,' he finally began, turning to face her, still holding her wrist in his grasp. 'Too often, things go wrong because of a simple misunderstanding——'

'You've got a nerve—calling this a simple misunderstanding!'

'—and we're too important to let this happen to us.'

'We're *nothing*,' she told him, her voice shaking with painful rage. Until a few minutes before, she had thought they were something—possibly everything—and she'd been sure that the only things that could happen to them would be good. 'There's no *us* for anything to happen to!'

'Jenny, Jenny...' his voice deepened, his hand loosened its grip, his thumb beginning to stroke lightly against the pulse-point at her wrist ' . . . you know better than that.'

'I don't!' Quickly, she snatched her arm away from his insidious touch, shifting the Best in Show award she'd been clutching with her other hand, now holding it against her body like a shield. 'I thought I did, but onlybecause you sweet-talked me and lied to me and played your games on me . . . and all that time you were in with Ralph and plotting with him . . . He was your partner!'

'He wasn't my partner——'

'Did you think his threats wouldn't be enough?' she demanded, totally ignoring his interruption. 'Did you think the only way to make sure you got my car was to make love to me? It really isn't that hot a property—Ralph should have explained that to you. The two of you didn't have to go to nearly such extremes—or is that how you usually do business? Do you always sleep your way—or *try* to—to get what you want? Is that how you became the great Grand Prix driver?'

'Jenny, I love you.'

'Ha!' She stood poised on the edge of hysteria, determined to harden her heart against his appeal, then discovered that she didn't need to make the effort. Her heart was already hard, a cold weight in her chest. 'Don't give me that!'

'I love you, and I knew nothing about what Ralph was doing—had done—to you until after you offered to sell me your car.'

'Of course,' she agreed sarcastically, now very cool, her emotions under better control with every minute which passed. 'You're paying him a finder's fee—and don't try to deny it, because I heard you say you would—when he had absolutely nothing to do with our agreement. That's a bad way to do business, Lucas. It's incredibly stupid!'

'Ralph has been working for Wes,' Lucas explained, stubbornly ignoring her outburst, as he had everything she'd said, Jenny noted, nursing yet another grievance against him. 'He and Carole decided that I ought to have a car, and Wes asked Ralph to help me find one. I was willing enough to go along with the idea—I had nothing compelling to do, and at least an antique was something

to do with cars without getting back into the high
pressure of what I'd been doing.'

'I really don't care about that,' she said coldly.

'But I'm trying to explain,' he snapped, finally taking
notice that she'd said something. 'Ralph told me he knew
someone who might have an old Franklin for sale, that
the owner had had business reverses and probably needed
to raise ready cash. He claimed that the owner would
sell, once Ralph provided a little persuasion, and if
enough cash was offered. He also said he was pretty sure
the owner would be at this meet, that he'd find out if
the car was for sale and let me know. But the point is
that Ralph never told me exactly what the car was—no
year or model. *More* to the point, he never told me the
owner's name, never even used a pronoun, come to that.
I'd have remembered if he'd ever said ''she'' when we
were discussing the matter. If he had——'

'You'd have figured that you didn't need Ralph to pull
off the deal,' Jenny supplied sarcastically. 'I suppose you
don't think there's a *she* alive who can resist you.'

'For heaven's sake, Jenny! I'm trying to explain that
I am bright enough to put two and two together. If I'd
had any idea that Ralph's prospect was a woman, I'd
have realised that it probably was you as soon as we
met. As it was, though, we'd already talked and you'd
taken me for that first ride—something had already
happened between us—before Ralph came to tell me that
he'd talked to the owner and it looked like there might
be a sale.'

'Because he'd cornered me when I went to my room,
and told me about the sordid things he'd been doing,'
Jenny observed, her voice clear and cold. 'And you
expect me to believe that he didn't tell you anything about
his talk with me?'

'It's the truth,' Lucas insisted. 'Even when we met for
dinner and out of the blue you offered me your car, I

still didn't connect you with Ralph. My only thought was that if you really did want to sell, I'd rather buy from you than through him. He's the kind of person I don't like or trust.'

'You're going to pay a finder's fee to a man you don't like or trust,' she scoffed, clutching her plaque a little more tightly.

'Look, I knew Wes wasn't the world's best judge of character, but I was willing to go along with him, and that meant doing business with Ralph. I had no idea you even knew him, much less that it was your car he was trying to sell me, until you explained the whole thing to me at dinner.'

'At which point you very carefully kept your mouth shut,' Jenny pointed out with icy calm. 'You said nothing about knowing him.'

'How could I?' Lucas asked with a brief gesture of appeal. 'You were so hurt and angry about what he'd done to you—and rightfully so. What could I have said?'

'You could have told me the *truth*,' she shot back, no longer cool, no longer in control. To think what these two men had done to her, first Ralph, then Lucas—the two of them together, plotting and scheming...'All you had to do was tell me the truth—something I expect you don't know much about!'

'Would you have listened?' Lucas asked quietly. 'Or would you have reacted just as you are now?'

'Well, you'll never find out, will you?'

'No, it's too late for that, but last evening was too soon. You didn't know me well enough then; you wouldn't have believed my explanation. At the start, I could sense your doubts and reservations——'

'And I was right, wasn't I?'

'—so how could I have expected you to believe me before you even knew me? It was an incredible mess——'

'Well, you're right about that,' she bit out. 'It still *is*!'

'—and I thought the only way out was to say nothing until we knew each other a little better——'

'Until you had me eating out of your hand,' Jenny corrected, knowing that if she didn't maintain her anger, she'd *die*—to think of what a fool she'd been! 'That way, you could get the car *and* have a bit of fun with me for the weekend!'

'I never wanted a bit of fun with you for the weekend,' he shot back, finally goaded beyond his endurance, she guessed. 'I wanted *you*! I still do, but it seemed best to wait until you knew me well enough to trust me when I told you I'd had no idea——'

'Ha! Butter doesn't melt in your mouth, does it? You'll try to talk your way out of anything.'

'Jenny, I didn't even *want* your car after you told me what Ralph had done! Instead of agreeing to buy it, I offered to loan you the money.'

'A nice touch,' she scoffed. 'If I'd had any reason to doubt you, you laid it to rest with that offer.'

'I *meant* it,' Lucas insisted, but she was already turning away, suddenly sick of the battle—heartsick, she supposed, but she couldn't admit that yet. 'You're the one who turned me down on that. I tried——'

'Yes, and you're still trying, aren't you?' she enquired, her voice shaking in spite of her best attempts. 'But it didn't work—more fool I, for not calling your bluff and accepting your offer.'

'It still stands,' he put in quickly. 'The loan is still yours—no strings, no conditions, no sale of the car. Whatever you want, Jenny.'

'What I want,' she said clearly, briefly turning to face him again, 'is for you to get out of my life!'

'But not like this, Jenny,' he appealed, reaching for her. 'Please, don't let this spoil things between us. Let's work something out.'

'Go to hell, Lucas Lambert,' she told him, and when he took a step towards her she released the hardwood plaque, sending it sailing—like some bizarre frisbee, she thought as she watched it fly through the air—in his direction. Before she heard it hit the ground and then skitter a little further, she had turned her back on Lucas and was running for all she was worth—back towards the inn, then through the people still thronging the lobby.

They were going to think she was crazy, she realised when she saw the curious stares. For her to come back alone, after what Lucas had said just a few minutes ago... They must all be dying of curiosity, but she wasn't about to enlighten them. All she wanted was the sanctuary of her room, where the world—and especially Lucas—couldn't get to her.

When the door was safely locked behind her, she instantly burst into tears. Just nerves, she tried to tell herself, even as she cried her heart out, knowing it was far more than nerves. It was hurt and sorrow and the terrible sense of what might have been... if only Lucas had been an honourable man, not the rat, the skunk, the unprinc led bastard she now knew him to be. As bad as Ralph ever thought of being, she grieved, burying her face in the pillow to muffle her sobs. Worse than Ralph, because he had never done anything so cruel as to make her fall in love with him. Trust Lucas—the smooth operator—to do that to her! Damn him! she whispered. Damn him to hell... and then a fresh bout of weeping overtook her.

It was late—how late she had no idea—when she finally regained enough of her composure to be able to think clearly again. When she did, she knew only two things—that she hated Lucas Lambert so much that she never wanted to see him again, and that the only way to accomplish that was to leave the meet now. If she waited until morning, she was bound to see him; he'd start his arguments all over again, and that she couldn't bear.

No, she'd leave now—and why not? she thought, already throwing her things into her small suitcase. There was nothing keeping her here. She'd paid for her room when she'd registered for the meet; she could leave as soon as she had the car loaded, be on the road well before dawn and have much of the driving done before the real heat of the day. Even better, she reminded herself as she pulled on jeans and a fresh T-shirt, she'd be home early, before her mother became too worried about her. On this end she'd miss Lucas and, on the other, spare her mother some pain.

Outside, once she'd crept through the sleeping inn, it was, she guessed, the chill hour before dawn. The sky was no longer deep black, but faintly lighter and streaked with pale threads of grey. The moon, if there had been one, had long since set, and the cars on the lawn were like ghostly relics of an earlier age.

A world out of time. The thought came unbidden, and she cursed herself for remembering anything Lucas had said to her. That's over! Forget it, forget *him*! she lectured herself as she hurried to the spot where she'd parked the car the previous afternoon. But it wasn't there, and she stopped dead to stare uncomprehendingly at the place where it ought to have been.

A mistake. You chose the wrong row, she tried to convince herself, standing irresolutely in the shadowy darkness, wondering whether to turn left or right. It couldn't be far. She distinctly remembered that she'd had to park at the end of the lawn, so——

'I thought you might try something like this.' The spectral voice spoke out of the darkness, then a black form detached itself from the shadows. Even as she fought the first start of panic, Jenny knew there was no mystery about who had been waiting for her. 'Planning to leave without saying goodbye?' Lucas asked pleasantly.

'Where's my car?' she demanded, ignoring his question. 'Did you steal it?'

'No. I've just sent it on its way home, with Wes's driver doing the honours.'

'Then you *did* steal it! You had *no* right,' she told him, her voice shaking with all the anger she'd thought had washed away with her tears. 'I told you the agreement was off. I'm not selling my car to *you*!'

'Well, that remains to be seen,' he objected mildly, and in the darkness he lifted the suitcase and then her handbag from her frozen fingers, 'but I'm not taking it away from you—not yet, anyway. When I said it was on its way home, I meant to your place. I don't have a home.'

'Poor little rich boy,' she jeered. 'Trying to play on my sympathies?'

'I would, if I thought it would help,' he admitted cheerfully, 'but somehow I don't think you're yet at that point. Still, there's plenty of time. Come along, Jenny. We've got a long trip.'

'*We?*' she repeated. 'We're going nowhere! Let me have my things!' She grabbed for her handbag, thinking to get out her keys and run for the truck. Instead, she found Lucas's free arm clamped around her, her body drawn close to his as he started them both across the lawn. 'Let me go, damn you,' she ordered, trying to push herself free. 'You can't *do* this . . . just *take* me!'

'Ah, but I can, and I will,' he assured her, sounding amused—damn him!—and calm and unhurried. 'The truck is gone, but even if it were here you're in no shape to drive yourself all the way back. I bet you've had no sleep at all.'

'And you have, I suppose?'

'No, but that doesn't matter. I'm used to this kind of thing.' They were on the drive now, his footsteps sounding clean and purposeful, hers scattering gravel as he literally dragged her along. 'My car's just around the bend, as I didn't fancy manhandling you all the way down to the car park.'

'I'll run away,' she threatened, still fighting him. 'You can't make me come with you!'

'Want to bet?' he asked without rancour, not stopping until they reached the black Jaguar. Then he dropped her things to use both hands on her shoulders, turning her—none too gently—to face him. 'Jenny, there's no point in fighting. You've got no choice, no other way to get home. Your truck has a three-hour start on you——'

'I'll take the bus!'

'Not without money,' he told her, 'and I'm not about to let you have your purse. You're stuck with me, like it or not.'

'Which I don't,' she snapped, staring defiantly up at him. 'I don't know what you hope to accomplish by all this, but it won't work!'

'All I hope to accomplish right now is to get you home in one piece. The rest we can sort out after that.'

'No, we can't.' But when he released her, she didn't move. Where could she go? she wondered hopelessly. Into the woods? Hide there until morning, then try to borrow the money to get home? But Lucas—even if he didn't find her in the woods—would still be here in the morning. He'd figure out some way to stop her then, which meant that there was nothing she *could* do! He'd already won this round, she acknowledged, feeling incredibly weary and spent. There was nothing she could do, so she stood by the car, watching as he locked her suitcase and handbag in the boot before he came back to open her door.

'Get in,' he said quietly, but even in the pale darkness she could see the hard glint in his eyes.

If she didn't, she knew he'd do it for her. He'd lift her in, she'd feel his hands touching her again. Being dragged down the drive had been bad enough; she didn't think she could bear it again. Shivering—reaction and the chill of the night, she supposed—she climbed into the car. By the time he'd gone around to get in behind the wheel, she had turned away and curled up, facing the window.

'I'll never forgive you for this,' she said as he started the car, 'not for any of it.' Even to her own ears, her voice sounded empty and flat. Where was the rage? she wondered, trying to summon at least some energy and failing miserably. 'I hate you.'

'I know. I don't blame you, after the way Ralph set both of us up.'

No, that's not right, she thought, closing her eyes against a sudden filming of tears. You and Ralph set *me* up, that's what hurts—not what Ralph did, which is no great surprise, but that you were a party to it. I believed in you, trusted you ... even thought that I loved you ... Jenny Wren, won't you ever learn? Nothing changes. It's always the same, and for him it's all been just a game, and I was the pawn ...

'Jenny? Time for some breakfast.'

She awoke stiff and groggy, and stumbled after Lucas into one of the characterless rest-area restaurants on the Mass Pike. There, in the cheerful clatter of normality, she drank three cups of reviving coffee, pushed eggs and bacon around her plate, and hardened her heart against his drawn features, the grey pallor beneath his tan.

That's his problem, she thought, sitting in stony silence. She hadn't asked him to do this to her; she'd have been far happier—well, less unhappy, she conceded—to be going home on her own. She made another stab at her eggs, refusing to meet his eyes, refusing to wonder why he was still bothering to play the game when it must be obvious—even to someone with an ego as large as his—that he couldn't possibly win. Perhaps he still thinks I'll believe him, she speculated as they got back into the car for the second half of their trip, but he's in for a big disappointment. Not as big as mine was, when I found out what he'd done to me, but a disappointment none the less. That's one way—the only way— I can pay him back. That's all I have left of my self-respect, and my self-respect is all I have left. He's taken everything else—he and Ralph have, between them.

The car isn't sold after all, she realised, and if I don't sell it fast, the business will be gone. Once the business is gone, I'll have a hard time finding another job. All I know is how to restore antique cars, and who will give me a job after what Ralph has done to my reputation? I won't be able to support Mother, and she won't be able to stay in the house. Those two will have ruined her life and mine, and I will *never* forgive Lucas for that!

'There. Satisfied?' she asked coldly when she'd guided him the last twenty miles between the New York Thruway and the small town tucked into the rolling hills. They had finally reached the old brick mill building by the river to find her truck and its trailer waiting beside the shop, the driver lounging sleepily in the sun. 'You can leave now.'

'We'll unload your car first,' he responded grimly, and this time it was his turn to move stiffly when they got out of the car. 'So you can be sure it's all there,' he added in an attempt at his usually lighter approach.

'All right,' she snapped, too tired to put up a fight now, watching in stony silence while he and the driver rolled the little car out of the trailer and pushed it into the shop.

'Here are your things,' he told her, unlocking the trunk of his car to take out her handbag and suitcase. 'And this,' he added, coming up with the Best in Show award. 'You forgot this last night.'

'I threw it at you,' she reminded him. 'I don't want it back.'

'A little the worse for wear, I'm afraid,' he observed, fingering the dents and scars in the wood while he ignored what she had said, 'but perhaps it can be repaired.' He held it out to her, and when she made no move to take it he bent to lean it carefully against the wall, by the door to the shop. 'Well, that's it, at least for the moment.'

'That's it forever,' she snapped. 'Would you please leave?'

'All right.' He capitulated, surprising her by saying nothing more, merely walking to his car and getting in, weariness apparent in every move he made. He waited there, looking neither left nor right, until Wes's driver had got in beside him.

Silently, her arms wrapped around her waist as though to contain an excess of feeling she dared not name, Jenny watched it all. Not until the car had turned out on to the road did she finally speak. 'And don't come back!' she yelled after the car as it disappeared from view. Then she burst into tears.

There was no need to hurry home. Her mother wouldn't be expecting her for hours yet, wouldn't begin to fret and work herself into a state right away, so Jenny sat for a while in the sun, occasionally wiping her eyes.

She told herself that she wasn't waiting for Lucas to decide to come back and try again. She told herself that she was waiting for him to come back only so she could tell him once more exactly what she thought of him. Finally, though, she admitted the truth: she was waiting for him to come back because, for the first time in her life, she'd fallen in love. She desperately—heart-wrenchingly—wished that things hadn't gone wrong between the two of them, and she was still wishing that Lucas would come back and make things right again.

If only there were some way to undo everything that had happened, some way to rearrange things so that Ralph didn't exist, some way to go back and start over with Lucas and without Ralph's scheming betrayal. But if it hadn't been for Ralph, she never would have met Lucas, she reminded herself. He wouldn't have bothered with her, wouldn't even have looked at her if he hadn't already been after her car. And she'd be better off without either of them, she told herself, trying to be objective and firm. She'd be much better off not thinking about them, not thinking about what they'd done to her...

She got up, locked the shop without so much as looking inside—too discouraging, she decided, too shabby and empty of work—and climbed into the truck for the short ride home.

'Darling, you're early!' Alma Howe exclaimed, her relief clear in the smile lighting her face as she came out to greet Jenny. 'But you look terribly tired.'

'I am. I left before dawn, to beat at least some of the heat,' Jenny told her, ignoring any mention of how she'd actually got home, avoiding any mention of the larger reality of Lucas Lambert. She couldn't tell her mother about him, Jenny knew, couldn't even mention his name. If Alma realised that a man had been pursuing her daughter, she'd instantly begin building castles in the air, and nothing Jenny could say or do would stop her. 'It's a long trip.'

'I know.' Instantly, a shadow passed over Alma's face. 'And to do it alone—without your father to help you with the driving...or Ralph,' she added in a small voice, casting a quick, uncertain glance in Jenny's direction. 'I'd have felt so much better if you hadn't been making the trip by yourself, if there had been someone to help and keep an eye on you.'

'But it all went well, Mom,' Jenny assured her, thinking how much her mother would have approved of the high-handed way Lucas had practically kidnapped her and brought her home. 'And how about you?' she asked, determined to get the conversation away from a subject where she had to deal in outright lies or half-truths. 'Did you manage all right while I was gone?'

'Of course.' Her mother forced a quick smile, then turned away as her eyes began to fill with tears. 'It was strange, just at first, to be all alone in the house. It's the first time since——'

'Mom, you should have come with me.'

'No, that wouldn't have worked,' her mother countered quickly, attempting to sound brisk and determined. 'It's high time I got used to being alone—you can't spend your whole life trying to keep me company, and besides——' she paused briefly, fighting the return of the wavering note in her voice '—I don't think I could have handled the meet without your father. That would have been worse than being alone here.'

Inside, her mother headed straight for the kitchen to put together a light meal for them to share. For a while, the conversation was easy and casual, all the loaded topics Jenny knew her mother was dying to get into left unspoken until they were seated at the dining-room table.

'I don't suppose,' Alma began, concentrating on the small task of adding sugar to her iced coffee, 'Ralph was there?'

'Well, he was,' Jenny said stiffly, and now it was her turn to avoid looking across the table, 'but we didn't see much of each other, and what we did——' She hesitated, remembering just how horrible Ralph had been. If she told her, Jenny knew her mother wouldn't believe it. Alma was so naïve that she had no idea how unprincipled, ruthless and cruel some men could be. All those years of marriage to Sam had protected her from any of life's grim realities. 'Well,' Jenny finally resumed, 'I think you could say that Ralph doesn't like me any better than I like him.'

'I suppose he wouldn't,' Alma observed, her salad forgotten while she stared fixedly at her glass, 'after the way you fired him.'

'Mom, I didn't fire him. It was just that when I knew there wasn't going to be money to pay his salary, I had to let him go.'

'Oh, money again.' Alma laughed nervously. 'It always seems to come down to money, which is so strange. We never had to worry about money when your father was alive. And I know you're doing your best,' she hurried on, sensing Jenny's interruption forming, 'and I'm not being critical, dear. It's just that I wish it could be easier for you. You work so hard, and you worry so much— yes, I know you do, even though you try to keep it from me. I just wish that you didn't have to be so tied down.

'You're so young, Jennifer,' Alma continued, and now she did raise her head to look almost defiantly across the table at her daughter. 'You ought to be having fun, meeting men, having dates——'

'Men again,' Jenny muttered.

'I knew you'd say that.' Alma offered an apologetic smile. 'I know you think I'm a hopeless romantic, and

I probably am, but a good man is such a help and a comfort...and I just want you to have what I had with your father.'

'There aren't many men like Dad,' Jenny reminded her, in sadness, not anger. She was remembering when, for just a short time, she'd thought Lucas might be that man for her—not that she'd been consciously comparing Lucas to her father. She hadn't even been thinking of her father then; she'd been too busy imagining herself head over heels in love with a man who she now knew was nothing—*nothing*!—like her kind and honourable father. 'The chances of my finding someone like Dad are practically nil.'

'Well, you never know,' Alma rebutted, suddenly optimistic. 'If not Ralph, there could be a stranger just waiting for you—someone to take care of you and solve all our money problems.'

'Not likely, Mom,' Jenny said more sharply than she'd intended. Her mother had struck a nerve with that comment about a stranger just waiting... She could almost have been talking about Lucas, and for a moment Jenny wished she could tell her mother all about him. In fact, she wished she could burst into tears and pour out all her misery and hurt. 'Look, I'm awfully tired,' she began again, getting up from the table and clearing her place. 'If you don't mind, I think I'll go to bed now.'

'But, darling, you can't,' her mother protested. 'It isn't even six yet.'

'I know,' Jenny called back from the kitchen, carefully rinsing her dishes and leaving them in the sink, 'but the way I feel now, I could sleep the clock around.

She did exactly that, and awoke the next morning feeling at least a little more coherent and able to deal with life. She wouldn't forget in a hurry the pain of Lucas's betrayal, but brooding on his treachery wasn't going to solve her more immediate problems. It was time to get on with life, so she went down to the shop as soon as she'd dressed in her customary work uniform of jeans and a T-shirt.

Once Howe Restorations had shared the old mill building with another small business, but the other had failed, leaving Jenny alone in the long, steeply roofed building beside the river. Usually she didn't even notice the boarded-up windows in the other half of the building, but today their empty desolation seemed to mock her, emphasising her own loneliness.

Don't give in to it! she lectured herself. You're not going to accomplish anything by feeling sorry for yourself. You've got to get busy—sell your car and start working on the ones Ralph sabotaged. Then you'll feel better about life, she assured herself, going into the small partitioned space which served as an office.

First she tackled the old manual typewriter, hammering out an acceptable ad for the car, spending most time thinking about what price to set. It was hard, trying to juggle the conflicting demands of a quick sale and a fair profit for herself. She *needed* this money to save the business; she had a pretty good idea of how much she needed, and the car was worth that. Still, there was the temptation to price the car too low, just to be sure of a quick sale—an immediate sale! Jenny thought with grim humour, contemplating the slim balance left in her bank account. Finally she decided on a realistically fair price, accepting the fact that she'd probably have to settle for slightly less when the bargaining was completed.

Next, she had letters to write to the four owners whose cars needed work done to repair the damage Ralph had done, and here Jenny had to be very careful about her wording. She couldn't actually come right out and say that Ralph was responsible for the problems, of course, but she could *hint*: 'It has come to my attention that the work performed on your car by one of my employees was not up to the usual high standards of Howe Restorations. That employee is no longer with me, and I would like to assure you that the same mistakes will not be made again.'

There, that sounded reasonably good, she decided, going over the words. She didn't name Ralph, but everyone would know who she meant. When that was coupled with her offer to transport the cars and do the work at no cost, the owners would be crazy not to believe her. Feeling decidedly better about the direction life was taking, Jenny had just finished the last of the four letters when she heard the sound of a car stopping outside.

Business? she wondered hopefully, getting up from her chair, starting out of the office.

'Hello, Jenny.'

She froze when she heard Lucas's voice, saw his tall, rangy form in the doorway of the shop, silhouetted against the bright sunlight beyond. Her lips, which had already been forming a smile, clamped tightly shut, and she thrust her hands deep into the pockets of her jeans as she silently stood her ground and faced the man who was the source of all her misery.

'Jenny, I've come about us.'

'There is no us.' she responded coldly.

'Then I've come about the car.'

'As far as you're concerned, there's no car either,' she snapped. 'I told you—the deal is off!'

'Sorry, Jenny, but I've got two pieces of paper that say otherwise.'

'I tore mine up,' she lied, realising that they were still carefully tucked into the purse she'd been using that evening, still in the suitcase she hadn't yet got around to unpacking. 'There's no agreement left.'

'Oh, yes, there is,' he corrected softly, and she watched his shadowy form as he produced two small slips of paper. He checked them both with elaborate pretence, then began to read from one. 'It says right here—"I, Jennifer Howe, agree to sell my 1904 Franklin..." Name your price, Jenny.'

'I won't,' she insisted stubbornly. 'I told you, the deal is off.' She stopped, and then, determined to drive the point home, continued with her second lie in as many minutes. 'I've already got another buyer. I can't sell to you—even if I wanted to, which I don't. Someone else is going to buy it.'

'But you won't be able to sell it, not for a long, long while,' he told her, sounding amused. 'We've got a written agreement. If you're not prepared to honour it, I'll have to go to court and get an injunction against you. That means that you won't be able to sell that little car to anyone until we get this thing settled.'

'You wouldn't do that!'

'Of course I would,' he assured her, still sounding amused—damn him! 'Jenny, I've got plenty of time on my hands, and nothing better to do with it than spend it in upstate New York, playing legal games. Besides, all the legal games will give me plenty of chances to see you, and—who knows?—you may just change your mind about me.'

'Never!'

'Well, you may feel that way now—I can understand why—but I'm willing to gamble and give it a try.'

'I'll—I'll claim that you used duress or undue influence, or something like that,' she threatened feebly, and he actually had the gall to laugh.

'Jenny, to do that, you'll have to get yourself a lawyer, and a lawyer costs money—which is something I know you haven't much of.'

'But you can't possibly win,' she tried again, wondering how to get through to him. 'It's just two slips of paper, after all, and they weren't even witnessed. No judge is going to take them seriously.'

'I expect you're right about that,' he agreed cheerfully, 'but it will take a fair bit of time and money to find that out and get the injunction lifted. Until then, you'll be stuck with a car you can't sell, and no way to repair the damage Ralph did to your reputation. In the circumstances, with no new work coming into the shop, you'll be between a rock and a very hard place.

'No, give it up, Jenny,' he advised, carefully tucking the two slips of paper back into his pocket and taking a few steps towards her. 'It will be better for you if you swallow your pride and let me buy the car. Name your price, Jenny.'

'Name your price...' The words echoed in her head, and then it dawned on her that she'd found the answer. She had agreed to sell the car at whatever price she set, and he'd agreed to buy for whatever that was. If she set the price too high—too impossibly high!—he'd refuse, and that would destroy their agreement. As simple as that! she marvelled, scarcely able to contain her smile of triumph. Just name a price beyond reason, and Lucas Lambert will be out of your life.

But what price should she set? she wondered, realising that it was the second time that morning she'd struggled with that thorny question. The first time had been a sincere attempt; this time, of course, wasn't, so... She drew a deep breath, remembering the first price she'd set, mentally adding a zero, and opened her mouth.

'Two hundred and fifty thousand dollars,' she heard herself saying, and the figure knocked her back on her heels. Two hundred and fifty thousand dollars for a 1904 Franklin? A quarter of a million? Absurd! Some antique cars sold for that much; some even sold for millions, but *not* a 1904 Franklin! She was asking at least ten times what her little car was worth—it was bizarre, outrageous, totally unacceptable...

Dear lord, she had him! Not even a filthy rich fool would pay that price for her car. A madman might, but Lucas Lambert was too clever to be mad! 'Two hundred and fifty thousand dollars,' she said again, beginning to like the sound of those words, liking—no, *loving* what she had just done to him. There was no way he would pay what she'd asked, so she was about to be free of him. 'That's my price.'

'Fine.' He nodded without hesitation. 'Do you want that in cash, or will a certified cheque do as well?'

CHAPTER SEVEN

LUCAS was mad—stark, raving mad! No one would seriously consider paying a quarter of a million dollars for Jenny's car; even someone like Lucas Lambert wouldn't pay that kind of money! Jenny was sure he was accustomed to getting his way, but this was too much! He couldn't want the car that much, and he certainly didn't want *her* that much.

'You're not serious,' she finally managed. 'You couldn't be.'

'But I am, Jennifer,' he assured her, his voice low and intimate, teasing at her senses. 'I'm just as serious as you were when you named your price.'

'But I *wasn't*! Serious, I mean,' she wailed, suddenly hot and cold by turns, wondering how she'd managed to land herself in a mess like this. By calling his bluff, of course, she admitted miserably, and now he's calling mine. He must know that I'm too honest to keep this up. I could *never* take that much money from him or anyone! 'Look, the car's worth only a tenth of that,' she tried again, fighting to keep her voice steady. 'I never intended...I was only trying to get rid of you.'

'I know that,' he allowed, sounding as though it was still just a joke to him, 'but it didn't work, did it? It will take me a couple of days to put together as much as that, but I'll be back—say Thursday morning. Will that be all right with you?'

'No, of course it won't! You're joking...aren't you?'

'You'll have to wait and find out,' he answered pleasantly, turning to leave the shop.

113

Of course he was joking, she told herself, trying to be calm. He was calling her bluff, that was all, scaring her out of her wits, making her squirm, paying her back for not falling at his feet. She'd seen the last of him now—or would have, once he got into his car and drove away. They'd carried the game almost too far—both of them—but now he would end it. She didn't need to worry about having a quarter of a million dollars dropped into her lap; the idea was laughable!

'One thing more...' He was back, just outside the door, a golden form in the sunlight. 'You forgot to say—do you want cash or a cheque?'

'Cash,' she said recklessly, but what did it matter? Both his question and her answer were meaningless, a joke...suddenly a sick, perverted joke. 'Just leave me alone,' she added, her voice finally wavering, then she turned away, standing motionless until she heard his car drive away.

She spent the next two days trying to convince herself that she had nothing to worry about. Of course she didn't! The two of them had been like children playing chicken, each one raising the stakes, waiting for the other to flinch, to withdraw, to call quits...neither willing to do it first. But Lucas *had* left, she reminded herself optimistically. He'd got in that one parting shot about how she wanted the money—that incredible, impossible sum!—but then he had left.

She had been the one to hold steady until the very end. She was the one who'd got the very last shot—a thought which no longer had the power to please her. The whole business now seemed too childish for words. She just wanted done with it all: with the game of chicken, with Lucas, with everything that could remind her of him.

Then what will you do if he does come back with the money? she asked herself, growing cold at the thought. He couldn't; he wouldn't; he mustn't! But if he did...lord, what would she do? But he wouldn't! Thursday morning would come, and her splendid isolation at the shop would remain undisturbed. There was no way Lucas was going to come up with a quarter of a million dollars for her little car—for *her*!

But what if he does? she asked herself at least a thousand times. Why hadn't she swallowed her pride and sold him the car for a sensible price? It would have been easier and less costly than placing the ads. Besides, if she truly wanted him out of her life—and she did!— selling him the car at a reasonable price would have been the best way to get rid of him...so why hadn't she done it?

'Temper, temper,' her father had used to say with one of his easy laughs when she'd worked her way into a rage over some real or imagined injustice. 'Jenny, my girl, you're too hot-headed for your own good. Some day you're going to find yourself in an awful mess because of it.'

Well, she hadn't—not yet, but she might on Thursday morning. But if he did come with the money, would it really be her fault? she asked herself in an attempt at defiance. After all, this was no *imagined* injustice! Ralph had done his best to destroy her business, and, while she was fair-minded enough to concede that Lucas had had nothing to do with Ralph's original plan, he'd certainly been happy enough to take advantage of it. Even worse, Lucas had amused himself at her expense, toyed with her, even nearly managed to seduce her. No, in the event that he did come back with the money, he'd be getting just what he deserved. But he wouldn't come...would he?

Jenny's nerves were stretched nearly to breaking-point by Thursday morning. It had poured during the night, and she'd been kept awake by her fears and the sound of the rain pounding down. Only after the storm had passed had she finally been able to fall asleep. When she awoke, she was past the point where a fresh, sunlit morning could help, particularly when she came downstairs to find her mother already up, looking drawn and worried.

'The rain—wasn't it terrible?' Alma observed, pouring coffee and handing one mug to Jenny. 'It kept me awake most of the night, and then I heard… Oh, Jenny, I don't know what we're going to do!'

'Do about what?' Jenny asked with a terrible sense of foreboding.

'There's a leak—a terrible leak—in the guest room. I mopped it up, and put a pail under it, but——' Alma sat down in one of the kitchen chairs, clutching her own mug with both hands '—what are we going to do, Jen?' she asked plaintively. 'I've been worried about it for months, sure I could feel a damp patch, but I hoped…'

'What? That it would go away?' Jenny asked gently, forcing a smile. She too had been worrying about that damp patch and doing the same thing—hoping it would go away, or at least not get any worse until the business picked up and there was some cash to spare. But there still was no cash, and what did roofing jobs run to these days? she wondered, in her mind a mental image of the stack of unpaid bills tucked away in her desk at the shop. 'What we do now is get it fixed,' she said firmly.

'But we can't afford that,' Alma protested. 'You know we can't!'

'We can't afford not to.' Jenny stirred her coffee, then took a sip. This wasn't fair! she thought, raging against the fates which had reduced them both to the point where a leak in the roof was a real catastrophe. 'The longer

we wait, the more expensive the repair will be. I'll call
Bill Minor today.'

'Does it have to be Bill?' Alma asked uncertainly.
'Couldn't you call around and get a few estimates? You
know Bill charges more than anyone else.'

'But his work is the best, Mom,' Jenny reminded her,
'and Dad always called him.'

'I know.' Her mother nodded unhappily, staring down
into her coffee. 'But, Jen, things are different now ... I
know money is tight, and I don't want things to be any
harder for you.'

How could things be any harder? Jenny wondered, a
wave of utter hopelessness washing over her. The whole
thing was impossible, the business would fail, they'd lose
the house and—— No! she told herself, and, as quickly
as the hopelessness had come, it was replaced by a feeling
of gritty determination.

Those things weren't going to happen; she wasn't going
to let them happen! She and her mother weren't going
to spend all their time worrying about money, and her
mother wasn't going to keep doing without all the things
that mattered to her, the way she had been these last two
years. Things *would* be better, Jenny assured herself, just
as soon as she sold her little Franklin and got the money
to turn the business around.

There was an almost cosmic irony here, she realised
suddenly. Here she and her mother were, worrying about
a leak in the roof when for the last few days she'd been
living in fear that Lucas would arrive today with more
money than she could possibly imagine. If she had any
sense, Jenny thought with her first real smile of the day,
she'd welcome him with open arms—*if* he came back
with all that money. Which he wouldn't, of course, she
reminded herself.

So—today, when he didn't, she'd mail off those ads
offering the Franklin for sale, and she'd increase the price

she was asking by a little, she decided in a reckless burst of optimism. Her mother wasn't going to do without her small pleasures any longer. The house, which had always been her special pride and joy, was getting shabby. After two years, during which no work had been done on it, there was more to it than just a leak in the roof over the guest room.

'I'm going to call Bill about the leak today,' Jenny told her mother, her mind made up, 'and while I've got him on the phone, I'll ask him about having his men paper a couple of rooms—the guest room for sure, because a stain is bound to show up in there. You decide which other room needs redoing the most.'

'No, Jenny! We can't afford——'

'Yes, we can,' Jenny interrupted to say. 'I should have told you—I've got money coming in soon, and there's no reason why we shouldn't spend it. Besides,' she coaxed, seeing her mother's doubtful expression, 'you like redecorating.'

Jenny reached out to cover her mother's hand with her own. She was realistic enough to know that money couldn't make her mother happy again, but it could help. Alma needed the fun and excitement of something different, of choosing wallpaper and paint, of watching her decisions take form as Bill's men worked on the house. 'It's settled, Mom,' Jenny told her, giving Alma's hand a quick squeeze before she got up from the table. 'I'll call Bill this morning and see when he can get his men started.'

'But, Jenny, the money——'

'Mom, don't worry,' Jenny called over her shoulder, leaving the house to go out and climb into the truck for the short trip to the shop.

For the last couple of days she'd been straightening up, making the shop neater and cleaner than it had ever been—why not, when there was no real work to be done?

she'd reflected. This morning, she worked for a couple of hours on the project, finally stopping to glance up at the clock.

Nearly ten, she noted, congratulating herself for having kept so busy that she hadn't even thought—much less worried—about what she'd do if Lucas Lambert arrived on her doorstep with a quarter of a million dollars. And this was the Thursday morning you agonised over, she scoffed, reaching for the telephone to give Bill Minor a call.

Predictably, he was out on a job, and his impersonal answering machine launched itself into an explanation of when he might return any calls. At the sound of the beep, she obediently left her name and number, adding, 'Our roof's sprung a leak, and I wonder if you could get back to me about doing a job to patch it. And while you're at it,' she continued, trying not to let show the nervousness she felt at the thought of spending money she didn't yet have, 'would you give me some idea of how much it would cost to paper a couple of rooms?'

'Spending my money already?'

'*You,*' Jenny breathed, her heart almost stopping when she heard Lucas speak. 'What are *you* doing here?'

'You know very well what I'm doing here,' he teased, advancing into the office, dwarfing the small space with his presence. 'I'm here to buy your car, and you must have decided to give in without any more arguments, or you wouldn't be launching a redecorating scheme. Although...' he paused consideringly, looking around '...given your asking price, I don't know why you're stopping at just two rooms. Why not have the whole place redone?'

'I'm not having anything done here,' she explained crossly. 'It's for the house. And I am *not* selling my car to you for that insane price!'

'Yes, you are, Jen,' he assured her, finding the only other chair in the room, turning it so he could sit with his long legs straddling the back, his arms resting on it. 'You are, as the saying goes, hoist with your own petard.'

'I'm not! You may be fool enough to be willing to spend that kind of money, but I'm not going to let you. Anyway,' she continued more easily, feeling an enormous sense of relief as it belatedly registered that he'd come into the shop empty-handed, 'you don't have any money with you, or did you decide to leave a quarter of a million dollars in the car?'

'What would you say if I told you I came in an armoured truck?' he asked very calmly. 'That the money is waiting outside with two armed guards?'

'You wouldn't!' She felt cold chills on her spine. 'You didn't!'

'You're right, I didn't.' He grinned engagingly, resting his chin on his crossed arms. 'It seemed more prudent to arrange to have it transferred to the local bank. It's waiting for you there, whenever you want to go down and count it.'

'Look, Lucas,' she began reasonably enough, fighting to maintain her poise, 'hasn't this gone on long enough? We're behaving like a couple of kids, and it's silly. I apologise for calling your bluff, and now, if you'd just stop calling mine——'

'But I'm not, Jen. The money is there, along with various bank officials who'll be considerably happier when you've taken a look at it and they can put it somewhere else. You see, banks don't usually keep that much money around, not as cash on hand,' he continued expansively, clearly relishing the moment—or her dazed expression—'and they can send it back to Syracuse by armoured truck as soon as we've opened an account for you. Come on, Jenny,' he urged, standing up, reaching across the desk for her hand. 'Let's go, so you can put them out of their misery.'

It was the shock, she supposed, that made her meekly follow him out of the shop, pausing only to close the door and snap the lock in place. It was shock or re-morse—an overpowering burden of guilt . . . 'Lucas,' she finally managed when they were both in his car, 'I *can't* let you do this!'

'Of course you can. It ought to be easy,' he told her, light-hearted, then relented enough to say, almost kindly, 'Look, if it's any consolation, I'm not giving you all two hundred and fifty thousand up front. Twenty-five thousand—that's what you intended to ask, isn't it?— will be yours this morning. The rest goes into an escrow account, and whether you get it, or how much you get, will depend on how well you live up to the terms of the sale.'

'What terms of the sale?' she demanded, instantly on her guard. At first, when she'd heard him say 'twenty-five thousand,' she'd felt an enormous sense of relief, but it sounded as though he planned to impose con-ditions, tie her up in something which would give him the chance to keep on tormenting her. 'There weren't any terms for the sale!'

'Well, there wouldn't have been if you'd asked a reasonable price,' he pointed out equably, 'but you de-cided to be clever about this, and two can play that game. But don't worry, Jenny. I'm not asking you to do any-thing illegal or immoral, and your lawyer will be at the bank to explain the terms of the sale.'

'I don't have a lawyer!'

'You do now—the one who used to do your father's legal work. Your good banker suggested him to me, as-sured me that this fellow had watched you grow up and that we could all be sure he'd have your best interests at heart. That's very small town, I suppose, but small towns are wonderful,' he observed with a reflective smile. 'I've never lived in one before, and it's amazing, the way everyone seems to know everyone else's business. It makes life so much easier.'

'For you, perhaps,' she said crossly, 'but not for me, when you take advantage of it. And just what kind of things are you going to expect for your money?' she belatedly remembered to ask.

'Nothing terribly hard,' he assured her, pulling into a parking space just down the street from the bank. 'I'd like to know a little more about antique cars, and I can't think of a better teacher than you.'

'*Me?*'

'That's right, Jenny.' He left her hanging until he'd come around to open her door for her. 'I'm buying your car, and in exchange you're going to educate me.'

'Isn't that tidy?' she observed, staring up at him, wondering how she'd thought she could win from someone whose mind was always working the way his did. 'Do you always get what you want?'

'I haven't always,' he answered, suddenly serious, 'but I'm going to this time. It's too important——'

'You're just playing games,' she scoffed as he touched her arm to direct her into the bank, 'but I can refuse to go along with you.'

'But you won't,' he assured her without any hint of a threat, but with considerable conviction. 'You won't be able to do it.'

He was right. Jenny knew it as soon as they stepped through the door of the bank. There were realities in her situation—the leaking roof, the sick truck, the lack of business, the terrible, grinding, unending need for money—and nothing drove the point home more convincingly than her glimpse of the loan officer who had been so condescending when he'd turned her down only a month before.

'Sorry,' he'd told her, not sounding sorry in the least, 'but your cash-flow position is awful. One might even say that it doesn't exist, and in the circumstances we can't make the loan.' That was all he had needed to say, but he hadn't been able to resist a couple of parting shots. 'I think, Miss Howe, you'd be better advised to sell the business before you run it into the ground. Why not take the sensible way out?'

'Because I'm not going to run it into the ground,' she had snapped. She'd sat silently, trying her best to behave like a lady during their interview, but she'd finally been goaded into responding. 'I *can* run this business, and I'm going to make it a success again.'

'I doubt it,' he'd told her, and this time he had broken into a smile, 'but if you're determined to try, let me give you one piece of advice. Don't expect the bank to bail you out each time you find yourself in financial difficulties. I realise that it's a temptation, certainly easier to depend on the bank than your own initiative, but it simply won't do. A loan to *you* will result in a loss for *us*, and we're in business to make money—something you'll have to do too, if you want to keep your business alive. Money, Miss Howe—that's the key. You really must learn how to make some.'

As if she hadn't already known that! she'd thought at the time, gritting her teeth, resisting the urge to pick up his pen and pencil desk set and throw it at him, at that smug and amused ferret's face.

Well, from the glimpse she'd caught of his face as she entered the bank with Lucas, the loan officer was no longer smug or condescending. There had been awe, chagrin and a certain degree of incredulity in his expression, and Jenny had felt a quick flare of vindictive delight. In that brief moment she knew—heaven help her!—that she couldn't turn down Lucas's offer.

Whether she liked it or not—and she probably wouldn't—her fate was sealed.

The branch manager showed her the stacks of money before they were whisked away to the vault, pending the arrival of the armoured truck. He explained precisely how the accounts would be handled, then deferred to her lawyer, who had gone over the terms of the sale agreement Lucas's lawyer had already drawn up.

'It's a very fair agreement, Jenny,' Mr Turner, who was an old friend of her father's, told her, 'particularly in view of the—ah—substantial sum involved. In return for such a sum, one might have expected Mr Lambert to extract considerably more from you in the way of concessions and commitments, but he's being eminently fair and not very demanding. In fact——' and here he permitted himself a dry little chuckle '—if I were *his* lawyer, I wouldn't allow him to go quite so far, give quite so much up for so little in return. But he has assured me that this is what he wants.'

At that, Jenny shot a quick and doubtful glance at Lucas, who—maddeningly!—merely smiled blandly back at her.

'All you're expected to do in return for the money,' Mr Turner continued, tracing his finger along the pertinent sections of the agreement, 'is permit him to work alongside you in the shop, for which you'll be compensated—generously!—at fifteen hundred dollars a day. In addition, you're being asked to maintain the car you're selling to him, and to participate in various meets and other antique car activities as directed by Mr Lambert, at the same rate of payment. These earnings, of course, will be in addition to the twenty-five thousand dollars you'll receive today for the actual sale of the car. The other amounts, as you earn them, will be transferred on a weekly basis from the escrow account to an active one in your name. Very generous, wouldn't you say?'

'I—yes,' Jenny felt bound to agree, but when she risked another quick look at Lucas she knew he was amused at the neat way she'd been forced into the admission.

'Now, the agreement has no expiration date *per se*, Mr Turner explained, 'but it does end as soon as payment for your activities has reached the specified sum. At that time, you may, if you wish, exercise an option to renew the agreement and continue to provide the same services to Mr Lambert at either the same rate of compensation as set forth in this agreement, or at some other mutually agreed upon rate. You're not bound to exercise your option, you understand, Jenny. You can, if you wish, simply walk away from any further dealings with Mr Lambert once you've fulfilled the terms of this agreement—which should take about a year or so, I estimate. However, I'd be remiss in my duties—and to the memory of your father—if I didn't recommend that you continue this bizarre but incredibly generous arrangement until such time as Mr Lambert—er——' Mr Turner hesitated, then smiled benignly '—until Mr Lambert comes to his senses. Provided, of course, that he ever does,' he added in a brief, puckish aside.

But he will, Jenny assured herself, even as she took the pen Mr Turner was offering her and signed the agreement. This business wouldn't last long—Lucas's interest in her wouldn't last long. Soon—*very* soon, she fervently hoped—long before the year or so was up, she'd be left in peace, but in the meantime she'd have the financial security she so desperately needed. Which was why—the *only* reason why, she assured herself—she signed her name to the papers.

'Are you hungry?' Lucas asked when the last of the details had been completed and they were back in his car. 'We could celebrate over lunch.'

'Is that in the agreement?' Jenny countered caustically, staring resentfully out through the windscreen. 'Have I got to?'

'No. I just thought you might like to.'

'Well, I don't,' she snapped. 'I'd like to go back to the shop.'

'Whatever you say,' he agreed so mildly that she shot him another darkly suspicious look. 'Don't worry, Jenny,' he told her, intercepting the look. 'Having gotten so much of what I want, I'm prepared to be patient.'

'What you want,' she exploded, turning to glare at him. 'That's all you think about—what you want! I should have guessed the first time I saw you. You're rich and spoiled and out for a good time—but I never dreamed you'd pick on me, or go to quite such lengths.'

'Neither did I,' he agreed with a wry expression, 'but events conspired——'

'You and Ralph conspired—not events! The two of you, planning just how to bring me to my knees...' A little dramatic, she conceded, but still... Just the idea, fresh and raw again, was enough to renew her feeling of impotent rage, and her hands curled into small fists, her nails digging sharply into her palms. 'Well,' she finally managed through the rushing fury, 'after what the two of you have done to me, you have only yourself to blame for spending all that money.'

'Oh, I don't care about the money,' he assured her cheerfully. 'I expect to get a good return on my investment.'

'Only in a business sense,' she said pointedly. 'Don't think for a minute that I'll do anything—anything at all—except what I have to do. I won't be nice to you, I won't see you socially——'

'Won't let me kiss you?' he suggested with a flashing grin. 'Won't let me hold you or——?'

'Won't do anything except what's in that damned agreement,' she broke in to say, her voice shaking with anger. 'How can you even think that I'd let you...? Knowing how I feel about you...and you tried to *buy* me!'

'No, Jenny, not *you*,' he corrected, briefly serious. 'All I've bought is time.'

'Time,' she scoffed, tossing her head, missing his quick, appreciative glance at the way her dark curls tumbled around her face. 'Time to try to play your games with me? Time to amuse yourself until something more amusing comes along? Well, it won't work,' she warned him as they arrived back at the shop, and she grabbed for the door-handle the instant the car stopped moving. 'Just remember that—Mr Lambert,' she told him, scrambling out of the car, slamming the door behind her. 'I won't *let* it work!'

'I think you might,' he said reflectively, catching up with her while she fumbled with the key to the shop. 'There's something going on between us, Jenny. There has been from the start. You can't deny it.'

'I *can*,' she raged, whirling around to confront him, instantly wishing she hadn't. He was too close to her, too large, too formidable, and—touched by sunlight as he was—much too attractive. The elusive scent of cleanliness and citrus aftershave teased at her, and he was smiling down at her, the creases back, bracketing his lovely mouth... 'If you think,' she began unsteadily, that familiar breathlessness betraying her once more, 'that I could like you now...'

'I'm not sure "like" is the right word,' he teased, advancing on her, placing the palms of his hands on the door behind her, effectively holding her prisoner. 'There's always been something a lot stronger than "like" between us—you know that, Jennifer.'

'No,' she whispered, watching, hypnotised, as he bent his head. 'No,' she said again, closing her eyes in the instant when his lips met hers, coaxing, teasing, playing games with her senses until her knees threatened to buckle on her.

He was clever, she thought abstractedly, *much* too clever! He knew exactly when her resistance began to fail, knew when to gather her into his arms, knew when she couldn't help herself and had no choice but to melt into his embrace, knew when to part her lips and deepen that clever, clever kiss...

'You see?' he finally quizzed, withdrawing just enough to smile down at her dazed expression. 'The magic is still there between us. Jennifer, the magic is always going to be there for us... and neither one of us can do a thing to stop it.'

'But I can try,' she whispered unsteadily, after he had got back into his car. She leaned limply against the door to the shop as she watched him turn on to the road. 'I have to; I *can't* let him do this to me... Oh, lord, what *can* I do?' she asked the sunlit sky, then shocked herself by bursting into tears.

CHAPTER EIGHT

'JENNY, darling! Where have you been?' her mother called, out of the house as soon as she heard the truck turn into the drive. She paused briefly on the porch, then came down the steps, smiling and effusive. 'Darling, you should have *told* me!'

Had Bill Minor already been in touch with her mother? Jenny wondered, sliding wearily out of the cab of the truck. He must have been, because Alma was happy now, while Jenny felt emotionally battered. It had been an incredibly difficult day, and now she was bone-tired, wanting nothing as much as a hot bath, her supper and bed... and what *was* her mother chattering about?

'...so nice, when you might have told me he was doing all those terrible things. I——'

'Who?' Jenny demanded. 'What are you talking about?'

'Why, Ralph, of course,' her mother explained, as though to an idiot child. 'I can't believe it! He fooled me completely.'

'How did you find out?' Jenny asked with a sudden sense of foreboding. 'Who told you?'

'Lucas, of course,' Alma answered promptly. 'Such a charming man, so unlike Ralph, and he showed me the agreement you signed, so I know that *he* isn't lying to me.'

'You've talked to him?' Jenny asked with ominous calm. 'He came here today?'

'He's still here. In fact, he'll be staying with us until he gets a place fixed up for himself here in town. He and I have been having a delightful conversation, and it seemed natural to invite him, and I think he rather hoped I would. The poor man has never had a proper home, and he needs looking after, nourishing meals...and we've been waiting supper for you,' she added, finally remembering. 'Come along, dear.'

With only that brief warning, Jenny was forced to face Lucas again, forced to face him and the whole incredible mess he'd made of her life. All through dinner and the seemingly endless evening which followed, she nursed her grievances.

Bad enough, she fumed, that she would have to spend every day at the shop with him, but there wouldn't even be the prospect of a reprieve in the evenings. He'd be around all the time, and, if this evening was anything to go by, it was going to be even worse than she'd imagined.

It was Ralph all over again. First Ralph, now Lucas, drawing her mother out, giving her an excuse to fuss over dinner, flattering her, listening to her endless chatter as though every word mattered. As Ralph had, Lucas was treating Jenny with a kind of distant but courtly respect—just the sort of thing to give her mother ideas, Jenny brooded. Her mother had instantly switched allegiance, and Jenny was willing to bet that when she and her mother were alone the talk would be all about Lucas—Lucas, the answer to all their problems; Lucas, the wonderful man, 'So much like your father...Jenny, do try to be *pleasant* to him!'

And then, because Jenny knew that Lucas and Ralph were two of a kind, the days at the shop would be more of the same. Like Ralph, Lucas would go out of his way to be helpful, try to take the worst of the load from her shoulders, want to share with her the day's trials and small triumphs. Like Ralph, Lucas would do his damndest to insinuate himself into her life and make himself indispensable.

Yes, it was going to be Ralph all over again, but with one devastating, terrible difference. She had thought she was falling in love with Ralph, but now she knew that she hadn't been. There had been nothing of wanting, of desire, with Ralph; those feelings in her were something new, something Lucas had taught her. She'd have to cope with those feelings every day while she worked with him—'the magic', he called it, but to her it was a curse, something she had to learn to control.

She would grow a hard shell, she decided as the evening continued, the three of them now drinking their coffee on the veranda, where the soft summer darkness at least made it impossible for her to see his face. Still, it was sheer hell to sit there, rigid and wary in one of the old wooden rocking-chairs, while he talked with her mother. Jenny was locked in a terrible struggle with herself, trying to resist the allure of his voice, deep and seductive against the light counterpoint of the crickets and the fitful stirring of leaves by the soft summer breeze. Yes, she was going to have to grow a hard shell around her emotions—and her physical response, she acknowledged with brutal honesty—and she would have to do it quickly.

But the shell wasn't yet in place when her mother stood up, announcing her intention to go off to bed. Like a shot, Jenny was on her feet too, determined not to be left alone in the darkness with the source of all her troubles.

'I think I'll——'

'Not so fast, Jenny.' A hand like a steel cuff closed on her wrist; Lucas, lounging apparently at his ease in the rocking-chair next to hers, had just struck again. 'Before you go up, we'd better clear the air.' Inexorably, he forced her back into her chair, his hand resting with deceptive gentleness on her wrist once she was seated again. 'I know you're not happy to have me staying here, but I want you to know that it wasn't my idea. Even I wouldn't have dared push my luck quite that far. Your mother made the suggestion, and she seemed so pleased by the idea that I hated to hurt her feelings.'

'Of course,' Jenny agreed sarcastically, 'it's that altruistic streak of yours—always trying to consider other people's feelings.'

'And here I was, thinking you never give me any credit,' he teased. 'It's good to know that you realise I've got a few redeeming qualities.'

'Don't push your luck, Lucas,' she said through gritted teeth, and he laughed softly in the darkness.

'All right, I won't, and it wasn't simply altruism that made me agree. A house—a real home—was enticing after all those hotel rooms——'

'Poor little rich boy,' she jeered.

'Besides,' he said, laughing again, 'I couldn't resist the chance to see you on your home ground, to see if I could figure out a little of what makes you tick. Already, your mother's been very helpful in that.'

'I'll bet she has!'

'You've been too good to her,' he said, ignoring Jenny's small outburst. 'It's obvious that you've spent the last two years doing everything in your power to shield her from the new realities. Jenny, your father is dead, and it would have been kinder to be cruel enough to let your mother realise how different things are now.'

'How could I do that?' Jenny demanded, forgetting that she owed Lucas no explanations. 'She'd already lost Dad. I couldn't make things even worse for her.'

'You could. You *should* have.' His voice came out of the darkness, firm and inflexible, almost angry. 'You should have been living your own life, and it's high time your mother had a chance to survive on her own. She's still young. She could make a new life for herself.'

'Of course! You know more about it than *I* do, I suppose,' Jenny shot back, indignant. 'What makes you think you can waltz in here and in just a few hours decide that I'm doing things wrong?'

'Because I can be objective and you can't. Besides, you have an absolute genius for making things hard for yourself—heaven knows why,' he mused, almost to himself. 'You've been struggling to keep the business going, trying to keep things the same for your mother, refusing to accept my help—but all that's going to change.' Still with his hand on her wrist, he stood up and turned to face her. 'I'm here now, and I'm going to make things easier for you.'

'I don't want your help! I just wish you'd go back to wherever you came from and leave me. *Stay away,*' she said frantically when his shadowy form bent towards her, his hands on the arms of her rocking-chair, forcing the chair forward until she was sitting bolt upright, her face only inches from his. 'Don't you dare touch me!'

'Don't worry, I won't—not until you're a little more...ready,' he said softly. 'We'll put that aspect on hold for a while, if that's what you want, but don't think you can put *me* on hold, Jennifer. I'm part of your life now—just as you're a part of mine—and that's not going to change.'

Jenny stole out of the house as dawn was breaking, thus postponing her next fraught encounter with Lucas. Yesterday's only bright note had been a telephone call from one of the men she'd written to about Ralph's shoddy work. The man, an old friend of her father's, had sounded relieved, had told her he'd been sure there was some logical explanation for the problems he'd had with the work done on his car in the shop. They'd agreed that she would come immediately to pick up the car and start the repairs, so Jenny had a perfect excuse to avoid Lucas for an entire day.

Or even longer, she began to think when the truck started running badly on the heavily laden trip back to the shop. 'The bad news, Miss Howe,' she told herself with wry humour, thinking out loud, 'is that you may be stranded on the New York Thruway, stuck for a couple of days while you try to get the truck running again. The good news is that, if that happens, you won't have to worry about Lucas for all that time!'

A tough choice, she mused as she nursed the truck through the twilight. She was inclined to think that she'd be grateful for any reason that helped her to avoid Lucas. On the other hand, she couldn't spend the rest of her life—or that portion of it Lucas was prepared to devote to tormenting her—trying to dodge him. On the whole, she concluded, it would be better to get used to his presence as soon as possible, steel herself against his clever assaults and develop that hard shell she was going to need.

In any event, the decision was made for her when she made it back to the shop, if only barely. You'll walk home tonight, girl, she told herself as she switched off the faltering engine and coasted into the area outside the shop.

Immediately, even with only the pale glow of a half-moon for illumination, she could see that things were not as they had been when she'd picked up the trailer that morning. The black Jaguar was parked in the yard, and by the door of the shop there was a large pile of what looked like construction materials—lumber and sections of metal scaffolding.

'What's all this?' she demanded of the dark shadow which detached itself from the wall to meet her. 'I didn't order anything.'

'But I did,' Lucas explained as she brushed past him to unlock the large door of the shop. 'This place is badly in need of repairs, so I made arrangements today to get them started.'

'Well, you shouldn't have,' she snapped, releasing the lock, forestalled in her efforts to push open the door when he did it for her. 'I don't own the place, and my lease prohibits any repairs without the landlord's permission. He could make things difficult for you.'

'I doubt it. I bought the building today, Jenny. I'm your landlord now.'

'No!' She switched on the lights, then closed her eyes briefly against their glare. In more normal circumstances, his news might have made her want to bang her head against the brick wall; now she was too dog-tired to do anything except long to sink to the ground. 'What is it with you?' she asked, brushing back her curls with one weary hand. 'You're spending money like a sailor on leave——'

'Perhaps that's how I feel.'

'—and driving me mad! You've got me trapped— you're all around, all the time. You're going to be at the shop every day, you're going to be at the house every night. Now you're my landlord and you're going to be doing things to this place... You've taken over my life... and I can't handle it,' she finished, her shoulders slumping as she turned back to the truck. 'Not now.'

'Yes, I can see that,' he agreed, looking down at her, studying her face with frowning concentration. 'Look, why don't you go wait in the car and let me take care of things?'

'I can——'

'Of course you can, but there's no need. Go, Jenny,' he ordered with such quiet authority that she surprised herself by doing as she was told.

'You need a new truck,' he told her when he'd finally completed the job of getting the trailer inside the shop and had locked up and come to join her in the car. 'That one's living on borrowed time.'

'It only needs a tune-up, and maybe new rings.'

'It needs a damn sight more than that,' he told her, switching on the Jaguar's engine, which promptly emphasised his point by purring like a kitten. 'See that you get a new one.'

'Or you'll do it for me, I suppose,' she said with a flicker of the old resentment. 'Hell! Are you ever going to stop trying to manage my life for me?'

'Probably not,' he admitted cheerfully, 'although I promise to do it only when it's absolutely necessary.'

It didn't take Jenny long to find out that Lucas's definition of 'only when it's absolutely necessary' meant most of the time. Even though she was up before six the next morning, he'd beaten her to the bathroom and was already at work in the kitchen by the time she'd showered and dressed and made it downstairs.

'Your mother says you never bother with breakfast. That's a poor way to start the day,' he informed her as, in a marvel of timing, he lifted the last of the bacon from the frying-pan as she entered the room. 'Since you've made it clear that you don't want her to get up this early for you, the job falls to me. You can start the toast,' he directed, draining the bacon fat, then pouring beaten eggs into the pan.

'Sorry to disappoint you, but I only want coffee,' she told him, ignoring the toaster to pour herself a cup, wishing he hadn't made it. It was only six in the morning and already she was obliged to him, although she had to admit that fresh-brewed tasted better than the instant she always made for herself. 'I don't like breakfast.'

'I can't believe that.' He stirred the eggs, then reached past her to start the toast. 'Everyone likes breakfast, except for a few pregnant women, I suppose. It's such an inoffensive meal, and it's good for you. Here, eat up,' he instructed, dividing the eggs between two plates which he put at the places he'd set at the table.

In doing so, he leaned near her and she caught the clean scent of the soap he'd used, saw the way his hair, still damp from his shower, curled darkly against the back of his neck. Like her, he was dressed in faded jeans and a T-shirt, the first time she'd seen him dressed so informally. He was playing at being just like everyone else, she thought, not able to find it within herself to be as derisive as she wanted to be. When he moved past her again for the toast, she couldn't avoid seeing the way smooth muscles bunched beneath the confining knit of his shirt, or the way his faded jeans had moulded themselves to his powerful thighs.

'So how does a poor little rich boy learn to cook breakfast?' she jeered, needing to find some way to avoid thinking about spending all day with this incredibly—impossibly—attractive man. 'I thought you never had a real home.'

'I didn't,' he answered so coolly that she guessed that her question had struck a nerve. 'The closest I came was with a cook we had for a couple of years when I was a kid. I spent as much time as I could in the kitchen, and I suppose I learned by osmosis.'

A couple of years, Jenny thought, feeling properly chastened, starting to eat as a way of atoning. 'Then she left?' she asked inadequately.

'Not by choice.' There was a definite edge to his voice, and he looked away briefly. 'My parents decided that it wasn't fitting for their child to be spending his time in the kitchen with the hired help. Since they couldn't fire me—much as they must have been tempted—they fired her.' Then, before Jenny could offer even the lamest of apologies, he continued in a very different tone, 'So, what do I help you do today? Do we work on that car you brought in last night?'

'Mmm. It threw a rod—one of the cars Ralph fiddled,' she explained between mouthfuls, taking Lucas's lead. 'We've got to take down the engine and see exactly what's wrong.'

She'd sealed her fate with that '*We've* got to take down the engine', although she didn't realise it immediately. By the time he'd been there a week, though, she had begun to acknowledge the magnitude of Lucas's presence in her life, and to wonder just how she'd managed without him.

She had to admit that it was helpful to have a spare set of hands, someone to hold the light close when required, someone to help with the heavy lifting, someone to pass tools to her when she leaned deep into an engine. If Lucas had done nothing more, that would have been enough to earn her grudging gratitude; as it was, though, he brought considerably more to their work.

'How do you happen to know so much about cars?' she asked at the end of that first week, a week in which he'd come up with any number of helpful suggestions and good ideas. Then, realising just how silly her question had sounded, she quickly continued, 'I know you've been driving race cars for years, but that's not the same as working on them, and race cars certainly aren't like antiques.'

'But the same principles apply—you know that,' he pointed out, then favoured her with the odd, twisted smile she now knew so well. 'Or you would if you weren't so everlastingly sceptical about everything about me. A fuel pump's a fuel pump, and the internal combustion engine always works more or less the same way...and you don't seriously think I spent all those years just showing up in time to get in the car and go out and drive, do you?'

'I don't seriously think anything about you,' she snapped, wishing they weren't working quite so closely as they bent over the Pierce Arrow's engine, wishing the day weren't so hot and heavy that it had made perfect sense for him to strip off his shirt. Now, standing back for a moment to ease her own aching back, she was presented with the broad expanse of him—the smooth, deeply tanned skin, the play of powerful muscles as he wielded a wrench. It was enough to make her want to reach out and touch him, to rest her hand on his shoulder and savour that strength. 'I try not to think about you at all,' she finished crossly, ignoring the truth.

'Just my luck.' He glanced back over his shoulder at her, with that same odd, twisted grin. 'Ah, Jenny, can't you see? I'm doing my damnedest right now, hoping that you *are* thinking about me…that you'll at least be willing to give me a chance.'

'I think——' She stopped, fighting the sudden dryness in her throat, the sudden close intimacy of the moment. Which was absurd, she reflected, because how could there be any intimacy with Bill Minor's work crew swarming all over the building?

That was something else to hold against Lucas, she reminded herself, trying to summon some indignation and failing miserably. Now that he owned the building, he was sinking what had to be an enormous amount of money into it. The work was another example of the way he was taking over her life, what with rewiring, putting in a new heating system, replacing old windows and doors in the shop. He was even converting the loft area overhead into living space for himself; he'd made her go up once and see how Bill's men had raised dormers

on the side overlooking the river, had even had the nerve
to ask her if she liked it!

How could she like it? she had wondered, studying
the large space with its slanting roof lines, the views of
the river and the woods on the other side. Her first
emotion had been envy; she'd wished that she'd had the
idea first—and the means and the freedom to make this
light and airy space into a place for herself. How could
she like it when, while it would finally get Lucas out of
her mother's house, it would instead place him directly
over her shop? He was taking over her life, dominating
it to the exclusion of anything else, although sometimes
she wondered how much of that was his doing and how
much was simply her own lack of resistance to him.

'Jenny?' he prompted, recalling her to the present as
he abandoned his work on the Pierce Arrow's engine to
straighten up and face her. 'What *do* you think?'

'I——' Lord! What had they been talking about? she
wondered wildly. 'I—I don't know what to think.'

'Then how about thinking—believing—that I'm madly
in love with you?' he suggested softly, his words barely
audible over the sounds of hammering and workmen's
voices overhead. 'How about accepting the fact that
we're two of a kind, that, if any two people were made
for each other, we are. I knew it almost as soon as I saw
you that first day, and by the time that day had ended
there was no doubt in my mind. I knew you were the
girl for me, and I'm going to marry you, Jenny. There's
no other choice for me, and before I'm done you'll feel
the same way.'

'That's ridiculous! You're just playing more games,'
she said stiffly. He and Ralph were the two of a kind!
Lucas was making himself just as indispensable as Ralph
had, using her for his own reasons just as Ralph
had . . . and Lucas would hurt her just as badly as Ralph
had—no, Lucas would hurt her more, she realised, be-

cause Lucas mattered so much more. *Had* mattered, she corrected hastily, refusing to admit that he could still matter at all. She was still attracted to him—no use trying to get around that fact!—but the attraction was just a physical thing. No, Lucas didn't matter—he *couldn't*! She couldn't bear the pain of letting herself believe what he'd just said about marriage—not when the day would come when he'd tire of the game he was playing and walk out of her life. 'I think you'd tell me anything, if you thought it would do any good,' she said now, bending back over the engine, determined to break this new and dangerous mood between them. 'You just want to get your own way.'

'That's right, Jenny,' he agreed cheerfully, moving in again to help her with the engine, 'and what I want most is to make you see that it's *your* way, too.' Only then, when he'd got in the last word once again, did he finally let the matter drop.

'By the way, we've got some planning to do,' Lucas announced casually when they'd finished a long day's work. 'We'll be taking the 1904 on a tour at the end of next month. We'll be gone for at least two weeks.'

'For two weeks,' Jenny echoed, incredulous, trying to work out the implications.

It was hard to believe, but now, at the end of October, they'd been working together for nearly three months, and working together surprisingly well. Not that there hadn't been the occasional problems, she acknowledged, but those problems really had nothing to do with their working together. It was *being* together that created the problems, but even those hadn't been as bad as she'd expected.

It was true that Lucas sometimes flirted wildly with her or dropped, without warning, teasing comments about his plans for their future, about getting married—

ridiculous thought! Still, Jenny could count herself lucky—although she sometimes wondered why she didn't feel lucky—that at least he never went beyond talk. Except for a few brief, almost brotherly, kisses, there had been nothing about his behaviour to bother her.

What could and did bother her was the way she so often reacted to him, even when he did nothing to provoke such a reaction. There had been one memorable day when, after they'd pulled off a particularly difficult piece of work, he had celebrated by picking her up off her feet, swinging her around and around until she'd been dizzy. By the time he had stopped, she had been gripping his shoulders, and there had been a moment when he'd just held her crushed to him, their faces—their lips! she had thought—just inches apart. There had been an instant suspended in time while they'd looked deep into each other's eyes . . . and Jenny had waited for him to kiss her. If he had, she'd known in that instant, she could not have resisted; she'd felt, in fact, that if he'd made the first move, she would have gone up in flames.

Lucas, *do* it! she had urged silently, feeling an incredible sense of desolate loss when he'd carefully placed her back on her feet and then released her. To her sorrow and bitter disappointment—and, try as she might, there was no other way to describe her feelings about it—he had never repeated that moment.

So she couldn't blame Lucas for the fact that there were times when she longed, even ached, for his touch. It happened whenever she was alone, which had come to mean almost every evening during the last couple of months. Lucas had moved into his new quarters over the shop, leaving Jenny feeling unaccountably aimless, even lonely, at home, with only her mother for company. And only when her mother was there, Jenny acknowledged, because she wasn't even seeing much of her mother these days.

It had taken a while for Jenny to figure out why Bill Minor spent so much of his time personally supervising the work on the house, and why, even after the work was completed, he stopped by so often—'Just to check on things,' as he said. It wasn't until the first time Alma invited him to dinner that the pieces fell into place for Jenny.

Bill's wife had died five years before; he was only a few years older than Alma, and a thoroughly respectable, eminently suitable escort. As Jenny watched her mother with Bill, watched their friendship blossom into something that looked suspiciously like a romance, she could only be relieved. If her mother could be happy again, could even be falling in love again, it meant that she'd put Sam's death behind her. In fact, the only disadvantage of having Alma spending so much time with Bill was that it did create lonely evenings for Jenny.

There was plenty of time—too much time—to think about Lucas, to remember what it had felt like when he'd held her and kissed her. Even worse than the remembering, though, was Jenny's perverse tendency to want him to do it again...

But now he was suggesting a tour that would take at least two weeks, and she felt stirrings of doubt. Two weeks on a tour, two weeks of being together day and evening, two weeks of hotels, among mostly strangers... Anything could happen during two weeks spent like that! Look what had happened in just two *days*, back at that meet in the summer!

'Two weeks,' she said again, buying time, her mind busy with the need to find a way out. 'Lucas, I couldn't,' she told him, lighting on a valid excuse. 'My mother would never let me go away for that long.'

'Jenny, your mother won't even notice.'

Which was true, she acknowledged, but still...two weeks, and so *soon*, just at the end of next month. 'Lucas, that's the end of November,' she shrieked as the thought struck her. 'We'll freeze! There's no windscreen, no roof... Do you have any idea how cold you can get in that car in the winter?'

'But it won't be winter for long,' he explained cryptically. 'Come upstairs and I'll show you.'

'Well...' She wavered briefly, then decided that it couldn't hurt to find out what this tour was all about. Besides, except for that one time when there had been nothing but an unfinished shell, she'd never been up in Lucas's quarters. She had to admit that she was curious about what it looked like, how he lived, how he spent all those evenings she found so long and empty.

It was one large space, except for the efficiency kitchen tucked in under the eaves and a small corner partitioned off, presumably housing cupboard space and a bathroom. Otherwise, living, dining and sleeping areas were combined, with only low bookcase dividers to separate each space from the others, the whole thing decidedly, surprisingly Spartan.

A long harvest table, a couple of chairs and some open teakwood shelving comprised the dining area; an Eames chair and footstool and a long, low leather couch stood alone on a deep shag rug to make a living-room; the sleeping area was nothing more than a huge bed, one severely modern bureau, a large antique armoire and, incongruously, an impressively high-tech rack audio system. That was it, she saw with a certain wonder, except for a collection of packing boxes and numerous untidy stacks of books, magazines and papers.

'It's pretty minimal, isn't it?' he offered apologetically when he saw her assessing glance. 'I'm not really unpacked or organised yet, and I know I need more furniture, but I've been waiting——' Abruptly, he turned away to rummage in one of the piles on the floor. 'Yes, here it is.' He came towards her, holding out a slick, brightly coloured brochure, making it clear that she wasn't to ask what he was waiting for. 'What do you think of this?'

'Run to the Sun!' Jenny glanced at the bold print on the cover, absorbed the graphic of a vintage car parked in the sweeping drive of a posh hotel. Inside, there were more posh hotels, more vintage cars, a sketchy map and a day-by-day itinerary. 'On Friday evening,' it read, 'we assemble at one of the Pocono's grand old resort hotels for a gala send-off dinner. Bright and early on Saturday morning, we begin our "Run to the Sun" with a first easy stage...'

'Lord spare me this kind of deathless, breathless prose,' Jenny muttered, looking up at Lucas. 'Do you really want me to tell you what I think?' she asked, noting his pleased and expectant expression. 'Or would you rather tell me what you think?'

'I'd better let you go first,' he decided, gesturing vaguely towards the living area of the huge room. 'Sit down and tell me.'

'It's one of those pretentious tours for people with more money than sense,' she answered promptly, prudently choosing the lone chair. 'It's going to take almost two weeks for the cars to work their way down the coast, stopping each night for some high living at one outrageously expensive hotel after another, until the whole circus arrives at Palm Beach—*Palm Beach*,' she repeated. 'I don't know what could be more pretentious than that!'

'Well, I agree,' he assured her, his features alive with amusement, 'although the rest of my family wouldn't see it that way. We wintered in Palm Beach when I was a child; at least I did until school provided a convenient excuse to miss most of it. Carole and Wes still do.'

'And have you decided that you want to return to your roots?' she asked with an acid tone.

'Jenny, you know better than that—or you should,' he told her, grinning. 'What matters to me is that there's going to be a lot of publicity about this tour, and a lot of big spenders on it. Publicity and big spenders never hurt any business, and now that you've repaired your reputation you could profit from a tour like this. So could I, for that matter,' he added casually.

'How?'

'Well, as it happens, I've got a small business too,' he admitted reluctantly. 'It's involved in the design and manufacture of auto parts—only modern ones, thus far, but I've been thinking that we could expand into producing some of the more common parts for antique cars.'

'But I thought——' She paused, confused, remembering that first evening on the way home from dinner, when he'd told her a little about himself. Only a very little, of course, she remembered indignantly. He'd been careful not to tell her too much, not so much that he'd give away the little game he'd been playing! 'You said it was some kind of strange engineering,' she reminded him, still confused, wondering if he was playing a new game with her now. 'You said it was defence work.'

'No, that's the family business,' he corrected with that odd, twisted smile she was beginning to know very well, 'the business I wanted no part of. This one's my own—built with no help from my family.'

'But you never told me about it,' she accused.

'You never asked, and I didn't see any need to bring it up. It wasn't relevant——'

'Not relevant?' she demanded, all her doubts and sense of injustice returning. 'You've been playing around in my shop all this time when you had a perfectly good business of your own, and you don't think that's relevant?'

'That's right.' His smile was gone now; he stood on the far side of the shag rug, hands dug deep in his pockets, regarding her soberly. 'I wasn't even sure I wanted to keep it going, I hadn't been involved at all—it had been more or less running itself—since my accident. Call it irrational, but I thought cars were the last thing I'd want to work with again, which left a big question mark where my future was concerned.

'Then Wes and Carole nagged me into coming to that meet,' he continued, his hooded gaze fixed on her face. 'I met you, and discovered what an absolute joy an antique car could be. Instantly, I could see possibilities—in both you and the cars—and I wanted to learn more, do more, stay involved... For goodness' sake, Jenny,' he appealed, 'I didn't try to hide this from you! It just didn't matter, and you did... and then I began to realise that, unless I wanted to live off your work for the rest of my life, I'd better find some way to link up what matters now to what I already have. Believe it or not,' he finished abruptly, 'that's the truth.'

'But——' she started to object, then found—remarkably—that she did believe him after all '—you still should have told me,' she grumbled, to save face.

'Well, I just did, didn't I?' he pointed out, finally producing the ghost of a smile. 'Just think how much less you'd have liked it if I hadn't said anything to you and you heard it from someone else on this tour we're going to be doing.'

'True,' she acknowledged, unable to repress her own answering smile, '*if* we do go on this tour. Are you determined?'

'What do you think about it? Can your little car do it?'

'It's *your* little car now,' she reminded him, 'and of course it can do it, but it will be a David among Goliaths. The brochure says entrants are limited to cars 1915 and older, but no one is going to be crazy enough to enter something like a 1904 Franklin. I'd say it will be pretty much only the newest of the cars allowed—say, 1912 and up—and they'll be the big cars, the hot performers of the times.'

'All the better. Perfect, in fact.' Lucas finally left his spot on the other side of the rug to settle on the couch, leaning back with an expression of calculated satisfaction. 'Then the 1904 would stand out?'

'Like a sore thumb,' Jenny assured him, 'especially if it's really cold, or if—heaven forbid—it rains.'

'No problem. We'll invest in all kinds of the best foul-weather clothing—thermal underwear, waterproof suits... We'll be ready for anything.'

'Even so, you'd better hope that the tour is designed to let us run pretty hard until we get to the sun part, and those easy stages they talk about won't be easy for us, at least not until we get to flat country. They figure about——' she consulted the brochure again '—about a hundred and fifty to two hundred miles a day. In the Franklin, given hills and traffic and who knows what else, that probably means about ten hours a day—*if* everything goes well, which it probably won't.'

'Of course it will,' he contradicted carelessly.

'Sure, easy for you to say,' she observed resentfully, 'but you don't know what might happen on the route, and then there are mechanical problems to worry about.'

'No, we don't need to worry about the mechanical stuff,' he assured her, a gleam in his eyes. 'After all, you'll be there to make sure that everything goes well—and I have absolute confidence in you.'

'You think it's going to be as easy as that?'

'Oh, probably not,' he admitted, grinning, 'but still, Jenny... Jennifer, this is going to be *fun*!'

CHAPTER NINE

STANDING by herself, Jenny shivered against the bone-chilling cold of the first light of dawn, feeling more alone than she ever had in her life. It didn't matter to her that there were people all around: spectators braving the cold to watch this Run to the Sun begin, the tour officials, the mechanical and technical support people working on each of the cars. Nor did it matter to Jenny that her own car—what had once been her own car, she corrected quickly—was only a few feet away from where she now stood.

The car had stopped being hers, had lost its power to soothe and absorb her when Lucas had snatched it away in the summer; it was just that she hadn't realised how irrevocably she'd lost it until the previous evening. Until then, Lucas had been clever enough to make everything painless and easy for her. His enthusiasm had swept her along as they'd made their preparations for the tour. It was only when everyone had gathered last evening that Jenny had grasped the irony of their first conversation about the event.

All along, as they'd worked side by side, Jenny had thought that she and Lucas were in this together; even worse, she'd believed that something very special and real was growing between them. She hadn't realised how much he was keeping hidden from her, the games he was playing. There really was, after all, no difference between Lucas and Ralph. Like Ralph, Lucas had an ulterior motive for everything he'd been doing; it had all been for himself. She had—most emphatically—no place in his long-range scheme of things. But last evening... well, the evening had been an eye-opener for Jenny, and she supposed she should be grateful that she'd seen the truth before she'd been drawn in any deeper.

It had begun as soon as she'd left her room and gone down to the hotel's grand ballroom to join the festivities of the send-off gala. She had taken great pains with her appearance, had made time during the busy month of preparations to go into Syracuse and splurge madly on a white wool crêpe gown just for this evening. In her room, she had studied herself in the mirror and had enough self-confidence to think that the gown's simple lines set just the right tone of demure provocation. Given the closeness she'd thought was growing between herself and Lucas, she'd expected to see his eyes light with appreciation when he saw her.

Instead, he'd been almost distant when he'd hailed her and drawn her into the circle gathered around him. 'This is Jenny—Jennifer Howe,' he'd explained, making introductions. 'She's my technical consultant and navigator for the tour.'

'Not bad,' one of the men—Lucas had introduced him only as Hal—had observed, eyeing her closely. 'We'll be sure to get lots of photos of you and Luc in your driving clothes, posed in the car or working on it. You'll add some real sex appeal, which always sells well. I'm Luc's advertising manager,' he added carelessly when he saw Jenny's bewildered expression.

'Advertising manager for what?' she asked, and Hal had stared at her as though she were an idiot child.

'For the company,' he explained obscurely, and then, in the face of her continuing incomprehension, continued, 'for Luc Lambert Custom Line. Surely you know about it.'

'It seems not,' Jenny told him, wishing that Lucas hadn't turned his attention to the others in their small circle. She was already feeling lost and out of her depth; she could have used a little support. 'Do you mean his business?'

'Sure,' Hal agreed, and now it was his turn to look puzzled, 'if you call a company that size a business. We think of it as a *company*. Hasn't Luc explained it to you?'

'No,' she said coldly, determined that Hal—that no one—should see her mounting confusion and sense of panic. 'I'm really only along for the ride. Do you mind telling me what I'm supposed to help sell? Some auto parts, I suppose?'

'*Some* auto parts?' Hal repeated archly, then laughed. 'The whole range of auto parts is more like it—everything from carburettors to custom seats. We're one of the biggest independent parts suppliers in the field. Are you serious? Don't you know anything about the Custom Line?'

'Afraid not.' Jenny shrugged, clinging desperately to the remnants of her poise, dying a little inside as she remembered how casually Lucas had dismissed his 'small' business when he'd—finally!—bothered to mention it to her at all. 'My business is only with antique cars, and the older ones, at that. Anything newer than fifty years old doesn't interest me.'

'Right. That's the market segment we're moving into now.' Hal nodded emphatically. 'Luc said you'd be very useful for that.'

'Did he?' Jenny smiled, a meaningless, empty smile. 'I'm glad to hear it. Given all the money he's paying me, it's good to know I'll be useful for something.'

During the last month, Jenny had just about decided that Lucas was paying her all that money, not because he was a rich man willing to pay whatever it cost to amuse himself, but because she really did matter to him. That was what she had been letting herself begin to believe, but now, standing amid throngs of tour entrants, officials, friends, family and associates, she knew that neither reason was true. Instead, Lucas was paying her all that money because she could be useful to his company as it moved into a new market segment. Just like Ralph, she'd thought despairingly. She was nothing but an object, a means to an end, and the hurt was almost more than she could bear.

But there was worse to come. If any hope had been left alive after she'd spoken with Hal, it died for her when Lucas finally detached himself and her from the small circle of his company's executives to lead her to their table. There, waiting for him—certainly not for her!—were Carole and Wes, and someone else. Leigh was a willowy blonde, there for Lucas's benefit, Jenny realised as soon as she laid eyes on the beautiful girl in the elegant gown which made Jenny's white wool crêpe look like something bought off a rack in a discount store.

Lucas and Leigh—even their names sounded right together!—already knew each other; from the things Leigh said to him, it was obvious that they'd known each other for several years. Once they all sat down, it made no difference that Jenny was next to Lucas. Leigh was on his other side, and the two of them had plenty to talk about, leaving Jenny to nurse her grievances in silence or strained conversation with Carole and Wes.

To be fair, Jenny was forced to admit that Leigh seemed to be doing most of the talking, but Lucas *was* listening. He made no attempt to draw Jenny into the conversation; in fact, he ignored her completely. Which was understandable, Jenny acknowledged unhappily, all her insecurities once again upon her. Leigh was everything she wasn't. Leigh had beauty, taste and poise, an incredible sense of style; she had everything! She was also the kind of girl Jenny imagined Lucas had dated during his glamorous years on the Grand Prix circuit, the kind he still should be dating, if this evening was any indication.

The kind he *would* be dating in the future, Jenny learned later, when Carole drew her aside with the first genuinely warm smile she'd ever sent in Jenny's direction. 'I'm so pleased,' Carole murmured, gesturing discreetly towards Lucas and Leigh. 'It's obvious that the time he's spent working with you has done Lucas a world of good. Before that meet back in the summer, he was so closed off from all of us, so detached and isolated.'

She paused briefly, smiling fondly at the two just beyond Jenny, then continued confidingly, 'We were trying so hard to get him back into the swing of things, but nothing seemed to be working. Now I see——' again she paused, looking past Jenny '—that he simply needed a little time to himself, to sort things out, I suppose. Certainly it's a good sign, don't you think, that he wanted Leigh here for the tour?'

'That *he* wanted...' Jenny repeated Carole's words with the feeling that she was about to help drive the nails into her own coffin. '*Lucas* wanted Leigh here for the tour?'

'But of course,' Carole assured her with the silvery laugh Jenny remembered from the summer. 'Heavens! Don't you know my brother well enough by now to realise that I wouldn't dare force anyone on him? No, this was entirely his idea, and I couldn't be more pleased. I owe a great debt to you, my dear, for helping him get back to normal.' She placed one smooth and beringed hand briefly on Jenny's unadorned and rougher one. 'I'll have to see that Wes sends some business your way— as a way to pay you back for what you've done.'

'Don't bother,' Jenny said shortly, hiding something deeper than hurt. 'Lucas is paying me well for whatever I've done.'

After that, Jenny sat silent and nearly immobile until she saw her chance to slip away from the table and out of the ballroom, up to her lonely room. No one noticed her leaving.

So now she stood alone in the first light of the dawning, her arms wrapped tightly around her to ward off a chill deeper than that of the frosty cold morning. She hadn't slept much during the night, but none of her painful brooding had been resolved during her hours of wakefulness. It was all still there, a dead weight on her heart; she was nothing to Lucas but simple expediency.

From the very beginning of their relationship, he had been hiding the truth—several layers of truth—from her. It was bad enough that he'd hidden his true identity from her. It was even worse that he'd listened while she poured out her troubles with Ralph, when all the time Lucas and Ralph had been partners, or so close to partners that it made no difference.

Ralph was even here on the tour—just one more touch of salt for her wound, Jenny thought grimly. She had seen his name on the official list of entrants the previous afternoon. At the time, his presence hadn't bothered her. She'd still been believing in Lucas then, and believing in Lucas had meant believing his long ago explaining away of Ralph. It wasn't until the evening, when she'd finally seen the whole truth of how Lucas had been using her, that Jenny had become uncomfortably aware of Ralph. During that endless, unendurable dinner, he'd been seated a few tables away, watching her each time she'd happened to look in his direction. His gaze had been calculating and speculative—one which once would have bothered her. Now, it seemed only a minor distraction—nothing, really, compared to what Lucas had done to her. *He* had hurt her in a way which made Ralph's betrayal seem insignificant.

Lucas was using her to hype his business—a little sex appeal to boost sales as he moved into a new market segment. That was all she was, or ever had been, to him. His real world—his friends and family, his *romances*—was all wealth and glitter, where Carole and Leigh were completely at home, and Jenny was the stranger.

It didn't bear thinking about, Jenny knew, for all that she'd been thinking about it all night, was still thinking about it. There had been times during those long hours when she'd considered walking out, chucking the tour and Lucas to go home. Only her professional pride and the determination to salvage something from this whole painful experience had stopped her. Lucas might be nothing to her now, but there was still the business to think about. If he could use her, then she would use him to continue the rebuilding of her reputation by making sure that the little Franklin ran flawlessly all through the days and miles of the Run to the Sun.

So get on with it, she urged herself, finally moving forward to where the two mechanics Lucas had drafted were waiting for her by the car.

Except for the thoroughly modern headlights mounted on brackets at the front, the equally modern tail-lights and the two tyres lashed on the back, the car didn't look as though it was about to start on a journey of nearly fifteen hundred miles. Only she and Lucas knew how much thought and effort had gone into their preparations for the trip, how many spare parts had been fabricated in double-quick time and were now in their service vehicle, ready for any possible disaster. Yesterday afternoon, she had gone through the contents of the van one last time. Now, with Lucas at the brief drivers' meeting, it was her job to give the car its final once-over.

'You're going to be cold,' warned Ben, the younger of the two mechanics, as she joined them.

'Damn cold,' Harry added, his expression dour.

'That's the understatement of the year, I think,' Jenny acknowledged, flashing them both a broad grin. After all, it wasn't *their* fault that they worked for Lucas! 'Do you have any idea what the wind-chill factor is in a 1904 Franklin at speed?'

'No. What is it?' Ben asked eagerly, always wanting to pick up some new knowledge.

'I don't know either,' Jenny confessed, surprised to find herself laughing. This is a little more like it, she thought. It's better to keep busy, better not to brood. 'I've never needed to know before now. I wouldn't need to know now, if your fool of a boss hadn't been crazy enough to do this blasted tour.'

'But you're dressed warm enough—aren't you?' Ben asked, torn between doubt and belief.

'I wonder. Lucas may have faith in all this high-tech clothing, but . . .' She trailed off with an eloquent shrug.

'What they wear when they climb Mount Everest might do the job,' Harry observed drily.

'Too bad you didn't mention that to the man who pays the bills,' Jenny began with bitter humour, then all expression left her face as she realised that Lucas had joined them.

Abruptly, she turned away, busying herself with the task of checking the storage batteries under the seats, then looking into the boot to make sure they had spare oil, new spark plugs, all the other small parts they'd agreed they ought to have with them. Her tool-box was there for quick repairs, the kind she could accomplish without the delay of waiting for the van to catch up. The odometer and CB radio she'd added were in place, mounted on the dashboard in front of the passenger's seat, the oil reservoir was full, and the petrol tank . . . Knowing she'd already checked it several times, Jenny still did it again—anything to keep busy, to avoid facing

Lucas until the two of them were alone. Then she'd tell him exactly what she thought of him!

'Time to start, Jen,' he finally said, speaking just behind her bent form. 'Here's the map of today's route.' When she straightened up, he handed her the clipboard with its clear plastic cover. 'They had nothing new to report, except a brief patch of construction southwest of Reading.'

'Probably a water main froze and burst during the night,' she suggested tartly, wishing she hadn't when she saw his brief, appreciative grin. She didn't want Lucas appreciating her—not any more! That ought to be left in the past, where it belonged. Abruptly, she turned away, keeping her back to him until he had cranked the car to life and she was forced to climb in beside him.

He was driving because, as Jenny had pointed out to him, it was his car now, and he was the rightful driver. When she'd given him lessons on driving it, back in the warmer weather, she had discovered that, not only was he the rightful driver, he was the *right* driver for her little car. There assuredly was a world of difference between a Grand Prix race car and a 1904 Franklin, but apparently some of the same principles applied, because Lucas had almost immediately started doing things Jenny hadn't learned in ten years of driving. He knew, instinctively, it seemed, how to get maximum acceleration out of the car, how to combine spark and throttle for best effect, how to put this little antique into a pretty impressive drift on turns. 'Once a race driver, always a race driver,' Jenny had told him at the time, amused, and she'd been looking forward to admiring his efforts during this tour.

But not any more, she thought, sitting in stony silence as they were directed to the starting-point and their day's tour card was stamped. Finally, as the oldest car, they were the first to be waved away.

'So, what's wrong, Jenny?' Lucas asked, pre-empting her attack. 'You're coiled tight enough to snap now, and you walked out on me at the dinner last night.'

'I left you with Leigh,' she countered without thinking. 'You didn't seem to need *me* around!'

'Jealous?' he enquired smoothly, slowing for the turn from the hotel's drive on to the road. 'I know we go right here, but you'd better start checking directions for the next turn. Believe me, there are going to be plenty of them, because we're not exactly taking a direct route today.'

'Well, we've got almost five miles before anything happens. Just stay on this road,' Jenny informed him after scanning the sheet on the clipboard, 'and I am *not* jealous! I just wish you'd told me what to expect...' She hesitated, thinking quickly. 'All those management types from your company,' she improvised hastily— anything to keep him from seeing how deeply he'd hurt her. 'You might have warned me that you'd invited them.'

'I didn't invite them; they just came. I should have known, but I didn't give it a thought. They're only here because part of the purpose of this tour is to promote my business——'

'Oh, yes, that *small* business you told me about!' She turned to fix him with an accusing stare and a blast of frigid air struck her unprotected ear, reminding her how fast they were going now and how severe the wind chill must be. She pulled from her pocket the Balaclava Lucas had insisted she bring and tugged it on. 'You'd better put yours on too,' she suggested, forgetting for the moment her list of grievances. 'You'll get frost-bite.'

'Then steer for me, will you?'

She leaned sideways to take the wheel, acutely aware of him when her back rested briefly against his chest. 'About your business,' she resumed, glad to break the contact between them when he reclaimed the wheel. 'Why didn't you tell me that it's a large company, that you're so successful? That ad man—Hal—was looking at me as though I'm mildly retarded, because I didn't have any idea. I thought you were nothing but an ex-racing driver with a little tax shelter of a business on the side.'

'What was I supposed to say?' he asked reasonably. 'Oh, by the way, Jen, perhaps you'd like to know that I'm rich and successful, and I own a large company— which it isn't, not by my father's standards, or Wes's.'

'But it is by mine, and—— Oh! Turn here,' she yelled as she saw a landmark she remembered from the directions. 'I guess it wasn't five miles after all,' she added apologetically, then picked up the battle once again. 'And everyone knew but me.'

'Is that all that's bothering you?'

Of course that wasn't all that was bothering her! Leigh was bothering her; Carole's condescension—not to mention her view of Lucas's future—was bothering her. *Everything* about this tour, about him, about her, about them, was bothering her, but Jenny could tell Lucas none of that. She had her pride, after all—nothing but her pride, she reflected miserably, but at least she had that!

'Of course that's all that's bothering me,' she finally said stiffly, guarding both her tongue and her emotions. 'It's just one more thing you forgot to tell me, and I'm sick to death of all your lies and evasions... And now, if you don't mind,' she finished with elaborate politeness, 'I'd like to stop talking and concentrate on these directions.'

To her surprise and relief, he simply nodded, permitting her to withdraw into a silence as cold as the day, speaking only when there was a need to give him directions.

Their route, she could see from the map, was taking them generally southwest, avoiding any major population centres so that they could stick to the least heavily travelled roads. It was slow going for the little Franklin as they laboured up the steep mountain roads, although those times did at least provide a welcome respite from the worst of the wind. Then, when they would reach the crown of a hill, the wind would knife through them with breathtaking fierceness as they made the mad run down into the next valley.

So much for the high-tech clothing, Jenny thought more than once, but she was fair enough to concede that the clothing probably didn't exist that could keep them warm enough on a day this cold. Once, driving through a small town, they were forced to stop at a traffic-light. Glancing sideways, she saw the car's reflection in a store window—the little red toy, Lucas behind the wheel, she with the clipboard in her hands, neither of them identifiable because of the Balaclavas they were wearing.

'We look like a couple of terrorists!' she exclaimed, forgetting her anger in the moment of discovery. 'All we need are Uzis and a couple of hostages.' She stifled a giggle. 'People must think we're crazy!'

'Well, we are, aren't we?' he pointed out, and behind the unrevealing mask of his own Balaclava she thought he was smiling.

'And I suppose you still think this is fun?'

'Absolutely,' he agreed, 'and if it's fun now, just think how much better it's going to be when we're further south.'

'To be warm...' She sighed deeply, bracing herself for a fresh blast of cold air when the light changed and they started to move.

It was a relief, a little after one, to reach a check-point, to have a few minutes inside the heated van, a cup of steaming coffee clasped between her numb hands. By that time, nearly all the other tour cars had passed them. 'All the Goliaths,' Lucas had pointed out while Jenny had enviously watched them speeding by, with their windscreens to protect their passengers from the worst of the wind.

'They'll all be off the road, done for the day, before dark,' she wistfully observed. 'They'll be warm while we're still freezing.'

But the worst was still to come. The day, which had been growing increasingly overcast, finally turned downright surly. Somewhere west of Reading, heading into Pennsylvania Dutch country, they were hit with the first drops of stinging rain, and Jenny was goaded into swearing under her breath.

'Fun,' she muttered dispiritedly. 'You're sick if you think this is fun.'

'At least it can't get any worse now,' Lucas assured her, determinedly cheerful.

He was wrong. This was no passing shower, but a steady rain bordering on sleet, in a darkening world. Lucas switched on the modern headlights and they kept going, Jenny using a small pocket flashlight to read out the turns to him. Fifty miles left to endure, then forty... and then their van pulled in behind them, Ben commiserating briefly with them over the CB radio.

'You could ride with them,' Lucas suggested. 'You could guide me through the CB, and begin to thaw out and dry out. It's not that much further.'

'And miss all the *fun*?' she enquired with appropriately icy sarcasm. 'No, thanks! If I've stuck it out this far, I can stick out the rest.'

'That's my girl!'

Jenny heard the approval in his voice, felt the brief touch of his hand on her arm—and pointedly pulled away. During this long and miserable day, they'd managed to achieve some kind of truce, but that didn't mean the battle was over. Lucas was still playing his game, and she wanted no part of it, or of him. It was

time for him to go back to his rich and socially promi-
nent family, to his company and his business deals with
unprincipled cheats like Ralph, to his gorgeous, never-
a-hair-out-of-place, lovely Leigh! She was welcome to
Lucas; as for Jenny, she wanted no part of the man!
Since the moment she'd met him, he'd done nothing but
hide the truth and betray her, and she'd had enough of
all that.

Their stopping-point that first night was an old country
hotel. It was one of those places which had come close
to extinction before being fixed up so that yuppies would
find it quaint and charming, Jenny decided, determined
not to like it—or anything else—as she climbed stiffly
down from her seat.

Late as it was, a few of the tour participants and others
travelling with it had gathered just inside the hotel's
double front doors to watch their arrival. There was
Ralph, Jenny noted, pointedly looking away, only to see
Leigh come through one door to fling her arms around
Lucas. Heavens, she'll get her hair wet! What's the world
coming to? Jenny asked herself, refusing to acknowledge any emotion but scorn when she saw Leigh's
intimate gesture.

'Dear Lucas, we'd almost given you up,' Jenny heard
Leigh say, and she turned away in disgust.

'Harry, wait,' she called as he took Lucas's place
behind the wheel, preparing to drive the Franklin along
to the garage. 'I'll come with you to check everything
for tomorrow.'

'No, you won't.' Lucas had managed to disentangle
himself from Leigh, and now he firmly gripped Jenny's
arm, marching her into the hotel. 'What you need right
now is a hot bath and some food in you.'

'But the car,' she protested as he signed them in at the
desk, then headed them towards a broad flight of stairs.
'It's got to be checked.'

'Harry and Ben and I ought to be able to handle that. You've taught us a lot,' he reminded her, pausing in the upstairs corridor to unlock a door, 'and the car ran fine today.'

'But it won't keep on running fine if—— This is a suite,' she interrupted herself to accuse, instantly on her guard. There was an attractive sitting-room, a fire cheerfully blazing in the fireplace, and two open doors, each revealing the bedroom beyond. 'I am *not* staying in a suite with you!'

'I'm afraid you don't have any choice,' Lucas responded, and for the first time he sounded grim, or perhaps weary—from the day's journey? Jenny wondered, or had her new coolness finally got to him. 'The place is full, and we are not going to try switching rooms at this hour,' he bit out when he saw her next broadside forming. 'Now be a good girl and take a long hot bath, and then we can eat.'

'I won't eat with you!' She pulled herself out of his grip and turned to stalk towards the nearest bedroom. 'Go eat with Leigh. She's much more your type than I'll ever be! Just leave me alone.'

For good measure, she slammed the door behind her, then tried to put her anger behind her as she stripped off the layers of sodden clothing to step into a steaming hot bath. When she finally emerged from the bathroom, wrapped in a towel with another around her wet hair, she saw that someone had brought up her suitcase.

Well, she wasn't about to get dressed and go down to—to endure more humiliation at dinner, she decided, pulling out her flannel nightgown and her old woollen robe. She'd stay up here and have room service—Lucas could pay for it!—by the fire in the sitting-room, while he was downstairs, dallying with Leigh.

She called room service, ordered an enormous meal, then pulled a footstool close to the fire and sat warming herself, threading her fingers through her hair to help it dry. It was heaven, she reflected, to be warm and dry and about to have a good meal. It was heaven, too, to be alone for a while, and her thoughts veered sharply away from the idea of Lucas sharing a meal with Leigh. Why should I care what he does? she lectured herself, then stood up as she heard the distinctive rattle of a room service cart outside the door.

'Just a sec,' she called in response to the light tap on the door, but Lucas beat her to it, out from behind his closed bedroom door to open the one to the corridor. He was wearing his usual faded jeans and T-shirt, his hair damp and his skin glowing beneath what remained of his tan. She supposed he'd been soaking in his own bath while she'd been in hers. 'What are you doing here?' she demanded as soon as the room service waiter had departed. 'Why aren't you downstairs with Leigh?'

'That was your idea, not mine,' he retorted cheerfully, investigating the contents of the various dishes, heaping two plates with food and crossing the room to hand one to her. 'Here. Eat up,' he commanded.

'No, thanks,' she said coldly, ignoring his offering. 'I've already ordered a meal for myself.'

'This is it. I told them to double whatever you ordered—it's simpler that way.' Then, when she still didn't make a move to take the plate, his mouth tightened slightly. 'Give it up, Jenny,' he advised shortly. 'We're both tired and hungry, and as soon as we've eaten we can go over the route for tomorrow and get to bed.'

'All right.' Without a shred of graciousness, she took the plate from him, then the silver flatware and napkin he brought her.

If she hadn't been so hungry, she'd have refused to eat; as it was, she had no choice. Silently, she tackled the food, trying to ignore the sight of Lucas, sprawled at his ease in the chair nearest the fire, his long legs stretched out towards the warmth, the flickering flames casting strange shadows on his strongly boned face...

Stop it! she told herself sharply. Stop thinking about him, stop looking at him, stop wanting—— No! She *didn't* want Lucas; that was a mistake. She was so confused and unhappy right now that she wasn't thinking clearly; she was letting her imagination run wild, and that was no good.

'Before we turn in, we'd better go over the route for tomorrow,' he told her when they had finished their meal, and Jenny nodded obediently, forcing herself to concentrate when he sat down on the floor by her footstool, producing a slender gold pen to trace the dark lines on the map on the clipboard. 'They warn us that tomorrow will be more difficult than today was.'

'Not possible,' Jenny put in, and he grinned.

'I don't think they mean the weather. They're talking about our ability to stay on the route. There are a few places where it would be easy to go off on a tangent. One is here——' his pen stopped at the junction of several roads '—and another is here.'

His pen moved again, catching and reflecting the light from the lamp behind them, momentarily blinding her. Then the flash of brilliance was gone and she could see his fingers—those long, clever fingers—holding the pen lightly in their grasp, could see his arm with its lightly tanned skin and the fine golden hairs...

'...is here,' he was saying now, absorbed by the challenges presented by the route.

He had turned slightly, holding the clipboard so she could easily see it, and his shoulder, its hard-muscled strength clearly defined beneath his T-shirt, was touching her thigh.

'...be more check-points. What do you think? Jenny?' he asked quietly.

What? she wondered, staring at him, her eyes very wide. What was happening to her? She hated Lucas; she would never forgive him for the way he was using her, had betrayed her, so why was she feeling this way? There was something about his nearness, his strength, the absolute grace of him; she was beginning to feel things...

'Jenny?' He was looking at her, his eyes molten silver; she was losing herself in his eyes. 'Jenny,' he said again, his voice deeper now, sounding abstracted, sounding, she thought, the way she was feeling. 'Ah, Jenny... To hell with the route!' Half kneeling, he straightened until his gaze was level with hers, then captured her face between his hands, his palms on her cheeks, his fingers threaded through her tangled curls. 'Jenny... Jennifer, what's been wrong between us today? It can't just be the business, so why have you been so angry with me?'

'I—I haven't.' The lie was instinctive self-protection, the need to hide her feelings from him, but already those feelings were playing her traitor. The force of his attraction was too strong; his closeness was defeating both her anger and her hurt, but there was still her pride. 'Noth-nothing's wrong,' she finally managed, averting her eyes.

'Liar.' He slipped his thumb beneath her chin, tilting her head upwards until she had no choice but to meet his gaze. His eyes were a glittering silver, drawing her into their depths, and when he spoke his voice was a lazily intimate drawl. 'I think you really were jealous of Leigh, but that's nonsense. She bores me—always has—and you don't. You excite me, Jennifer Howe.'

Had she started this? she wondered distractedly as his lips touched her forehead, her eyes, the curve of her cheek. Had she started it or had he? And did it really matter? Did anything matter now, when the heat of his body was calling to hers, and his touch...? 'But you asked her to be here,' she attempted. 'Carole said——' 'Carole lied,' he told her, and now his arms were around her; he was holding her close, his lips like a feather on hers. 'Carole's afraid of you, afraid that I'll stay with you and never return to the fold, never be properly stuffy, socially correct and all that... But I don't want that,' he continued after a moment, and Jenny's world suddenly shifted when he drew her off the footstool to lay her down on the rug, her head cradled by his hands. 'I want you.'

'Then why——?'

'Forget about why, Jennifer. Let me kiss you.'

'But I'm afraid,' she whispered—afraid of the strange languor invading her, afraid of the heat of his body and the answering flame it was kindling in hers. 'I don't understand.'

'It's the magic,' he murmured, his lips closing over hers, searing her with his fire for an endless moment. 'The magic is still here,' he finally said, lifting his head to stare deep into her eyes. 'Can't you tell?'

'Yes,' she confessed on a long, drawn-out breath, her surrender complete, her lips parting, craving another kiss.

'Of course you can,' he told her, sounding amused, now withholding his kiss, his lips merely teasing at hers. 'You may be angry with me; you may even hate me, but you can't fight the magic.'

'I don't hate you,' she whispered, a further admission, but she no longer cared. Nothing mattered now but her need for his kiss and the weight of his body on hers.

Heaven help her, she was desperate for this, desperate for *him*, she admitted, her heart leaping wildly when his mouth finally recaptured hers. She'd been starving for this all those weeks when he'd been too much of a gentleman to even touch her. All those weeks when he'd been so *clever*, she realised suddenly, growing cold as she grasped the magnitude of his cleverness, how he'd led her to this point, denied her anything of himself until he'd been sure of her surrender.

'You're just playing a game,' she accused when, sensing her new resistance, he ended their kiss and drew back enough to see her face. 'You've been playing a game from the start!'

'Jennifer, this is no game.'

'Of course it is.' Defiantly, she stared up at him, fighting anger, a sick feeling of shame, perhaps even despair. 'You're just like Ralph!'

'So...' Lucas expelled a long breath, then drew slightly away from her. 'Is he what this is all about?'

'What this is all about,' she told him, on her dignity now, taking advantage of her freedom to scramble into a sitting position, 'is that I don't appreciate being used. You decided that I could be useful while your company moves into a new market, and I suppose—on a more personal level—that I've been a little diversion before you get on with your life—some fun with strange little Jenny.'

'Then something like this happened with Ralph?'

'Oh, not quite like this,' she taunted, glaring across at Lucas's grim expression, 'but only because he isn't as smooth an operator as you are. Subtlety isn't his style, but he hasn't had the advantage of your years of practice.'

'He was after the business?'

'Of course he was after the business!'

'And—what? He thought marrying you was the way to buy in?'

'He was practical; he *had* to be, because he didn't have all the money *you* do! Still, it's all just the same,' she continued, drawing her knees up, wrapping her arms tightly around them. 'He was after me for my business, while you're just after me for the boost I can give yours.'

'I'm after you.'

'I *know* you're after me! You've made that painfully obvious. What I don't understand is *why*. What's the attraction?'

'I love you.'

'Rubbish,' she snapped, furious with him because she *had* to drive away the pain of hearing him say what she'd once wanted so badly to believe. But it wasn't true—it couldn't be!—not when he'd lied to her and schemed with Ralph... This was Lucas Lambert—the great Luc Lambert, she reminded herself—and someone like that would never love someone like her. 'You say that to every girl.'

'Jenny, I've never said it before,' he told her gravely, with a sincerity that twisted a knife in her heart, 'and I never expect to say it to anyone else.'

'Rubbish,' she said again, but the pain was even worse now, threatening to bring tears to her eyes. 'I'm a diversion, and I don't expect I'll last very long. I'm the *hobby* Carole and Wes thought you should have—only you decided on me, instead of an antique car, but it's all the same. I'm pleasant and undemanding, someone to take up the slack in your life while you get back to normal after all those years of racing.'

'Not true,' he told her, then broke into a grin, 'and if you think you're undemanding——'

'Don't make fun of me,' she raged, but her voice was unsteady, and she leaned her head on her knees, hiding from that grin. 'Men have always made fun of me, and I don't think I can bear it again.'

'Oh, Jenny, Jenny...' Suddenly his arms were around her, and with a gentle but no less compelling force he drew her close. 'Why should men make fun of you?'

'Because I'm a joke,' she confessed, her tone tinged with misery and bitterness. 'I'm a tomboy, and not terribly attractive, and I'm strange because I've always liked cars. I'm that weird girl who works on old cars, and I've always been good for a few dates and a few laughs. It started in high school, and it never stopped,' she grieved. 'I thought it had with Ralph, but he was just the same... and then you... and nothing was any different,' she finished, then burst into tears.

This must be the final humiliation, she thought, even as she sobbed out her pain and her rage. He'd done this to her, driven her until she'd been torn apart by emotions she hadn't even known existed. He'd forced her into a corner, until she had no place to hide, until she couldn't hold back her feelings. Now that he knew how she felt, she'd never be able to face him again... and he was only making things worse. He was holding her gently but very close, his body swaying slightly as he rocked her, the way someone might comfort a child, one hand sweeping back her hair in a slow, soothing motion. 'I hate you,' she managed between sobs, her voice muffled against his shirt. 'I'll never forgive you for this.'

'Never is a long time, Jenny,' he cautioned gravely. 'Too long, I think.'

'Not for me,' she retorted through her tears, with none of her usual fire. 'I won't change.'

'Yes, you will,' he promised, still rocking her gently. 'Jenny, all men aren't the same, and even if some men have hurt you... Well, I never could. Just believe that, my love.'

There it was, she thought despairingly, that absolute, rock-solid certainty in his voice, sounding so real that it could almost convince her, but—'I can't,' she said on a sigh.

'But you could, and you will,' he told her, but for the first time he sounded as weary, as unsure of himself, as she felt. 'Jenny, my love, how long will it take you to learn to trust me?'

CHAPTER TEN

When Lucas rapped on her door the next morning, Jenny sat bolt upright in the darkness. Briefly, she was thoroughly disorientated, until she remembered where she was. But not, she realised with a dreadful clarity, how she'd got there. She could only remember that he'd been holding her while she sobbed her heart out; he had said something to her about trust, and then there was nothing.

Had she been too tired to remember going to bed? she wondered. Or—perish the thought—had she fallen asleep in his arms? Had he put her to bed? All she knew was that she was still wearing both her nightgown and robe; somehow she'd got into bed without any unnecessary delay, and she'd slept like the proverbial log.

Should she ask him? She pondered that thorny problem while she took a quick shower and pulled on fresh layers of foul-weather gear. 'I can't,' she finally announced to the impersonal room as she threw her things into the suitcase and checked to be sure she was leaving nothing behind. 'I don't want to know.'

She wanted only to forget the evening. She wanted it never to have existed. How could she ask Lucas when she couldn't bear to think about it? And yet, and yet... she couldn't rid herself of the memory of the way he'd held her, the gentleness of his touch and his voice. Those fragments—and that was all they were; she had been in such a state that only fragments remained— stayed in her mind as the Run to the Sun continued.

The day was as cold as the first, but without the torment of rain. Under fair skies they ran south, crossing the Susquehanna River somewhere south of Lancaster, finally entering Maryland west and well clear of Baltimore. Lucas had been right when he'd warned her that today's run would be more difficult. There were countless obscure turns, hard choices when three or four unmarked country roads met at a crossing, and Jenny was forced to concentrate on the directions, the map and her constant monitoring of the odometer she'd installed.

Being busy was the best thing that could have happened, she reflected during one very brief lull. Being busy meant that there was no possibility of really talking to Lucas. In the circumstances, with the end of the previous evening looming so large in her mind, the last thing she wanted to do was talk to him—a sentiment he seemed to share. Even when the day's run had ended at a small hotel just inside Virginia, he was uncharacteristically quiet, confining himself to no more than what was needed to be said about the car and preparations for the next day's leg of the tour.

To Jenny's relief, there was no cosy suite this night. Their rooms were on the same short corridor, but so, she discovered when she summoned the courage to go down to dinner, were the rooms of Carole and Wes and Leigh.

'We're going to stick with this all the way,' Wes explained when he saw Jenny's quick, startled expression. 'Wouldn't miss it for the world! Of course, we're going modern and by the direct route—none of this business of beating ourselves to death in the cold—so it makes a pleasant vacation. Carole and Leigh get in some shopping, time by the pool, even a chance to catch up on their sleep before each evening's little party.'

'Aren't they lucky?' Jenny murmured with an ironic twist. After a long day, buffeted by cold winds and the strain of being with Lucas, she wouldn't have minded the kind of leisurely day Carole and Leigh had enjoyed.

Instead, she endured nearly three hours of cocktails and dinner, forced to watch as Leigh flirted outrageously with Lucas, a process Carole and Wes regarded with approving smiles. Jenny would have liked not to watch, to avoid both the picture of Lucas and Leigh with their heads close together and the occasionally hard and cold looks Carole shot in her own direction. But to look away invariably meant to see Ralph, who seemed always to be looking at her. And always that same expression, Jenny thought edgily—that coldly speculative expression she'd seen the first night of the tour.

It worried her, as though she didn't already have enough to worry about. Ralph had something on his mind; he was thinking very hard about her, Jenny knew, repressing a small shiver. It stood to reason that he was angry with her. After all, she'd maligned his reputation, if only in the vaguest terms, when she'd written to the four men whose cars he'd sabotaged.

So Ralph was bound to be angry with her, for all that he seemed to have landed on his feet. He was on this tour, wasn't he? He'd found another fat cat; he was half of the team with the big 1913 Locomobile, so it wasn't as though she'd been responsible for putting him out of work. Besides, he didn't look angry so much as calculating—the way, Jenny suddenly realised, he'd often looked at her when he'd first come to work for her father. Then, of course, he'd already been planning to use her, so was he planning to use her again? she wondered uneasily. And if so—how? She didn't see how he could use her again, not after what had already happened between them. Surely Ralph was over for her; for all that he was staring at her, he was a thing of the past.

But Lucas was very definitely *not* a thing of the past. He might be as over for her as Ralph—and for many of the same reasons—but he was still very much a thing of the present. There were going to be more long days on the road together, more long evenings in one hotel after another—plenty of opportunities for Lucas to try something.

He wouldn't leave her alone for long—that she knew. He never did. He was always working at her, trying to find some new angle. She didn't mean anything to him— never had—but that had never stopped him. She could only suppose that she represented some kind of a challenge for him; he was determined—with the wilful determination of someone very spoiled—to . . . what? Have his way with her? Complete his conquest of her? Prove to her, to himself, to the world that he could have any woman he wanted—even one who had fought him as hard as she had?

Who knew what went on in his mind? Jenny mused, knowing only that there was one certain thing: before too long—surely before the tour ended—he would try something again.

But he didn't. The next three days passed as the second one had, in an uneasy but strictly businesslike accommodation between them. Each day, Lucas drove while she navigated, and there was really no chance for the kind of personal conversation she was dreading. Each evening was a repeat of the last, with Leigh monopolising his time.

No sense worrying about what he can do to me when Leigh is clinging to him like a limpet, Jenny thought more than once, sitting silent and withdrawn during the meal at the end of each day. That Lucas was at least as silent and withdrawn as she was was something Jenny was too wrapped in her own misery to notice.

At least the tour was beginning to live up to its name. They had spent one night in northern Virginia, and by the next were somewhere southwest of Richmond and Petersburg, poised just above the North Carolina border. The next day, the route cut east; they ran north of Greensboro, Durham and Raleigh, stopping somewhere near the ocean. By the next day, travelling through small towns and swampland, it was positively warm and very sunny. They ended that night at another old resort hotel, this one on the ocean, just inside the South Carolina border.

The next day would be their seventh, Jenny realised as she started down for dinner. The tour was half over now, and when it ended—what then? Would she ever see Lucas again, or would he go back to New York with Carole and Wes—and Leigh—and send some of his employees to close up his place on the second floor of the old mill building?

After all, once the tour was completed, he'd have accomplished what he'd set out to do. He'd have achieved the great publicity his company needed to launch itself into the antique car parts market. Throughout the run, Hal had been organising Press coverage, lots of photographs and video shots, and tonight, at dinner, he was waxing enthusiastic about how he would capitalise on the finish in Palm Beach.

'You've got such a lead now that I don't see how you can lose,' he observed with a self-satisfied air—almost, Jenny thought, as though he felt personally responsible for the car's smooth running and her and Lucas's combined talents at driving and navigation. 'Short of the car packing up, you're bound to come in first.'

'But I don't see how,' Leigh complained, fluttering lovely long lashes as she appealed to Lucas. 'How can you possibly win when you're always the first to leave in the morning and the last to get in at night? You can't be leading,' she finished positively, the matter settled to her satisfaction.

'There's more to it than time,' Lucas corrected, smiling—not, Jenny thought waspishly, at Leigh's naïveté, but simply because any man would probably smile when Leigh batted her eyelashes like that. 'There's a complicated formula—too complicated for you, pretty—that combines time with the age of each car. The older the car, the more time it can take to complete each day's run. If the car is old enough—which ours is—and if the driver and navigator do a good enough job—which Jenny and I are—then Hal's right. We almost can't lose.'

'Oh.' Leigh's features assumed a small, adorable pout; she paused, clearly searching her brain—which Jenny had already concluded wasn't too terribly large—for what to say next. 'But if you had a newer car, you'd get in sooner.'

'True,' Lucas agreed with a second smile, 'but if we had a newer car, I doubt that we'd be leading.'

'But would that matter so terribly much?' Leigh asked with a dazzling smile. 'It would give you more time to have fun—to lie around by the pool ... You'd even have time for *me*,' she finished triumphantly, with the sublime logic of the truly self-centred.

'True again.' Lucas nodded gravely, then shot Jenny a quick glance, his eyes alive with laughter, sharing a joke with her at Leigh's expense. 'The trouble with that line of reasoning, pretty, is that some of us think the time on the road is the fun. We enjoy the challenge—don't we, Jen?'

'Yes,' she managed, but only barely, because her throat was suddenly tight with the pain of that one glance. Lucas had pierced her heart with that glance, reminding her of what could have been—what *had* been until this meet had started, of what she had hoped for and wanted. *Still* wanted, she acknowledged as the conversation continued without her, and as soon as she decently could she slipped away from the table.

'Trust me,' Lucas had said. 'How long will it take you to learn to trust me?' The words echoed in her mind as she made her way blindly out of the dining-room, wavered briefly in the lobby before deciding against going back to her room. She'd had enough of impersonal hotel rooms; at the moment, she needed not only solitude but space, and the time to do some serious thinking.

Could she trust Lucas? she asked herself as she wandered outside. Could she, *should* she trust him? Had there ever been anything real between them, or had it all been lies? And what of Leigh, who was everything that she wasn't? It was true that Lucas hadn't been making any particular fuss over Leigh this week. In fact, while she'd been madly flirting with him, he'd hardly been reciprocating with any great enthusiasm. According to Carole, he'd wanted Leigh on this tour; he'd denied that, and his behaviour towards Leigh seemed to confirm his denial. It really didn't seem that Leigh mattered too terribly to him. On the other hand, Jenny admitted reluctantly, Lucas wasn't demonstrating that *she* mattered much to him either.

Ever since that night when she'd disgraced herself by bursting into tears, he'd been withdrawn and remote—because he'd been embarrassed by her outburst? Or was it because he'd expected to seduce her that night and was annoyed that he hadn't succeeded? Was he simply bored? Or—incredible as it might seem—was he waiting for her to learn to trust him? Did—could—Lucas possibly care about her after all? And how on earth are you ever going to find out for sure? she asked herself, finally turning back towards the hotel.

'Well, Jenny! Got a minute?'

Lord! Where had Ralph come from? Jenny wondered, starting as his broad form materialised out of the darkness of the cool, spring-like night. Had he been following her all this way?

'Funny,' he began, planting himself squarely before her on the narrow walkway along the sea wall, 'but we've been together on this tour for nearly a week, and this is the first time we've spoken. Have you been avoiding me?'

'No more than you've been avoiding me,' Jenny countered, wrapping her arms tightly around herself, suddenly cold. Or even a little frightened, she admitted, belatedly realising just how far she'd come. The hotel was a long way off, its lighted windows only barely visible through the ragged evergreen shrubbery which lined the landward side of the walkway. Suddenly, Jenny felt very alone, even exposed, in Ralph's presence. 'Besides, I don't see that we've got anything to say to each other.'

'I'd say we had plenty,' Ralph corrected with a slow smile. 'You've been doing quite a number on my reputation these last few months—something I could be holding against you. But don't worry—I don't,' he added with a geniality which rang false to her ears. 'I figure all's fair, as they say, and you didn't do anything more to me that I did to you when I had the chance.'

'But I didn't do anything, Ralph,' she pointed out, standing her ground in spite of her unease, 'except tell the truth.'

'Well, you fought back,' Ralph amended, all mellow reasonableness. 'You fought for what you wanted. You're like me, that way. We're both fighters, Jen. We're two of a kind.'

'I don't think so.'

'But we are.' He smiled again, trying to ingratiate himself, the attempt only serving to put Jenny more on guard than before. 'I did my best to ruin you, and now you've done your best to ruin me, so I figure we're even.'

'Fine. We're even,' Jenny agreed, wishing she could get back to the hotel. She wanted to put Ralph behind her, but the walkway was too narrow, the sea wall on one side, the untrimmed shrubbery on the other—too close, she thought uneasily. 'Let's just call it quits.'

'Well, that's not quite what I had in mind, Jen. What I was thinking is that maybe we ought to get back together again, at—— No, hear me out on this,' he put in quickly when he saw her involuntary gesture of protest, then doggedly continued, 'We ought to get together with the work. I could come back to the shop——'

'I don't want you back at the shop!'

'You're going to need someone at the shop,' he told her, still being very reasonable. 'Your business has already begun to pick up, so I hear, and it's going to get a lot better after this tour is over. You're doing great things for your reputation here, and the word's going to get around. So, you're going to need help at the shop, and you're not going to get it from that boyfriend of yours. He's going to call it quits with you, as soon as this tour is over. He will, you know,' he assured her, reading something—fear, denial, sadness?—in her face she hadn't known was there. 'He's already losing interest, now that he's got that willing little blonde along.'

'Ralph, I really don't want to hear any of this.'

'But you should, Jen, for your own good. You ought to think about taking me back because we always did work well together, even when we weren't getting along——'

'Even when you were deliberately doing bad work?' she enquired with distaste. 'Even when you were trying to ruin my business?'

'That wouldn't happen this time,' he promised. 'This time we'd be in it for the long haul. We'd be partners— well, not really partners, because you'd own the business. I won't try that twist again. This time you can count on me.'

'Never,' Jenny said coldly. 'I'll never count on you for anything.'

'Well, at least you could count on me not to do what Lambert's doing to you,' he offered with an unpleasant, knowing smile.

'Lucas is not doing anything to me,' she announced, drawing herself up to her full stature, very much on her dignity when she guessed what Ralph was driving at. 'Don't think that just because he and I are working together, there's something going on——'

'Hell, I don't mean that!' Ralph laughed broadly. 'Jenny, I *know* nothing like that is going on! I'd have known anyway, because you're not that kind of girl, but he's telling everyone who will listen that nothing's going on. It's a big joke to him—to everyone in there.' He nodded his head back towards the lights of the hotel.

'What are you talking about?'

'Don't you know? Don't you have any idea?' he asked, his voice dropping, growing gentler, almost...sympathetic, Jenny realised, suddenly cold all over. Improbable as it was, Ralph was beginning to sound as Tessa had when she'd come to Jenny's room to tell her Lucas's true identity.

'You don't know, do you?' Ralph said now—exactly what Tessa had said to her, and Jenny waited, her breath caught in her throat. 'Jen, it started at that meet back at the end of the summer. I'd told him I'd arrange for him to buy your car, but after he saw you that first time he told me to stay out of it. He said he'd get the car *and* have some fun with you. And I said, "Don't you believe it. She's one girl who doesn't play around." But——'

'Ralph, please,' Jenny managed weakly, but he ignored her.

'—he told me he'd make it where I'd failed, that he had a better line. "It's a challenge," he told me. "I like the chase.'' That's all you are to him, Jen—a *chase*, and at least with me you were something more than that.

'He's making jokes about you, Jen,' Ralph continued now, driving the point home. 'He's taking bets with some of the guys, saying that he hasn't scored yet, but he will before——'

'No!' Instinctively, Jenny put up one hand, warding off his words as though they were physical blows. 'Please stop!'

'But you ought to know, Jen.' Ralph took a step closer, his bulk interposing itself between Jenny and the lights of the hotel. 'You're being played for a real fool, and I think you ought to know it all.'

'I don't want to!' She shook her head, started to take a step backwards and felt Ralph's grip on her arm.

'Damn it, Jen, you're *going* to! You're——'

'She said she didn't want to.'

Faintly, over the pounding of her heart, Jenny recognised Lucas's voice. Then, in a moment's confusion, Ralph's hold on her was gone and she could see two shadows on the walkway. For an instant only, there was a strange kind of shadow choreography—Ralph's broad shadow and a taller, leaner one. Then there were noises— the solid sound of a fist on flesh, a painful grunt, the splintering of branches as Ralph's form collapsed into the shrubbery.

'Don't make me do that twice,' Lucas said evenly as Ralph clambered slowly to his feet. 'Just get out.' He turned, his back revealing nothing while he observed Ralph's retreat.

Finally, he turned back to Jenny. 'I heard,' he said after a moment, and his tone was different to Jenny's ears—precise and curiously empty. 'I heard...at least some of what he told you...' he paused to draw a careful breath '...and I suppose you want to know how much of it is true.'

'I——' Of course she did—*didn't* she? What Ralph had said had confirmed her worst imaginings; she *had* to know how much of it was true! Yet she hesitated, sensing something fragile now, a terrible waiting quality in Lucas's stance, in the way his shadowed eyes were watching her. 'How long will it take you to learn to trust me?' he'd asked, and now—finally—she *had* to think!

When they had been together, had Lucas ever given her any reason *not* to trust him? Had *he* ever hurt or betrayed her? Ralph had told her—but had Lucas ever done any of the things to her that Ralph had? Which one of them should she trust? That was one issue, but Jenny suddenly grasped the fact that there was another, deeper issue waiting for her.

Was *she* the only one with doubts and fears? Was Lucas immune to those emotions? If she asked him now to explain away Ralph's words, wouldn't that be its own sort of betrayal? Had the last few months meant nothing to her? Knowing Ralph, knowing Lucas—if she really *did* know Lucas, and that was the decision she would have to make!—how could she ask him to explain? 'How long . . . ?' he'd asked. *How long?* she now asked herself.

It was now or never; instinctively, she knew that. There was a leap here, and she would have to make it, or live with ashes all her life. 'No,' she finally said on a long, pent-up breath, 'I don't need to ask. Ralph was lying.'

'Are you sure?'

He didn't believe her. *He* didn't trust her yet—and why should he? Jenny asked herself. After all those months of her, and her doubts and fears and her distrust . . . why should he believe her now? 'Am I sure? Absolutely,' she told him, trying to cut through his careful waiting, trying to invest that one word with all the solid certainty she remembered from when he'd said the same to her. 'I'm not sure of everything, but I am sure of *you* . . . I think,' she added on a wavering note, but he had already folded her into his arms by that time, and she could feel, as well as hear, the quick, unsteady rumble of his laughter.

'Well, Rome wasn't built in a day either,' he observed, relief and lightness threaded through his voice, 'but that's a start. Oh, Jenny...Jennifer,' he murmured, then seared her with a kiss of such devastating hunger, need and passion that it left her clinging to him helplessly. 'My love,' he managed some time later, 'say you'll marry me.'

'Yes...if you're sure?'

'Of course I'm sure! Haven't I told you often enough? I was sure by the end of that first day——'

'But *how*?' she broke in to ask. 'How could you possibly know so soon?'

'Well...' He paused consideringly, smiling down at her. 'I was attracted to you from the start. You were a very foxy lady—*my* kind of foxy lady: graceful, sexy, clouds of dark, dark hair, a pretty little face, dark, snapping eyes...and not afraid to crank a car to start it. I was dazzled from the very start.

'And then it just kept getting better,' he continued, his smile growing reminiscent. 'You took me for that first ride and showed me that cars could be a gentler, better thing—that different world I talked about. It was certainly different from the Grand Prix world, all the noise and confusion and nervous edge, all the things I'd come to loathe. There wasn't any question after that. This was it, and *you* were it! The only trick was to try to convince you, while the most incredible series of things were going wrong.'

'Not telling me who you really were,' she supplied, searching his face, suddenly not sure again, 'and Ralph...and then about your company.'

'But I never lied to you,' he offered awkwardly, his embrace involuntarily tightening. 'There were—sins of omission, I have to call them—the things I didn't tell you. I should have been completely honest from the start. The first of it—not mentioning that I had a certain degree of mechanical knowledge——'

'A certain degree?' she repeated sceptically, feeling a little braver now. 'You have a *lot*—probably more than I do! Anyway, it was who you were—the fact that you were famous, and couldn't even be bothered to mention it to me—that hurt. That's what started all the trouble. I'd already been burned by Ralph. I was naturally inclined to distrust any man, and practically the first thing you did was give me a reason to distrust you.'

'But I didn't know that then,' he reminded her, 'and it was so much fun—you were treating me like someone slightly feeble-minded, about a subject where most people had considered me a minor deity. I was loving every minute of it—which only made things worse when you told me what Ralph had done to you.'

'Yes, Ralph.' She sighed. 'But you were right, you know. If you had told me that first night, I would have stopped things between us on the spot, and then you wouldn't have kissed me goodnight, and we wouldn't have had that next afternoon in the woods, when we had that picnic and then—and then——'

'Came perilously close to making love,' he finished for her when she broke off, blushing.

'Well—yes,' she admitted awkwardly, then summoned her courage to forge on, 'and I'm glad we did— what we did, because it was all new to me. I hadn't known...but I found out that afternoon just how important it was—and how much it meant to me. And I think—if that *hadn't* happened, there wouldn't have been *any* chance for us, after I found out about Ralph. Does that make any sense?' she finished doubtfully.

'I'm not sure.' He studied her face, a smile starting, slowly building to a grin. 'Are you trying to tell me that, even when you were hating everything about me, thinking that Ralph and I were two of a kind, you were too attracted to completely shut the door on me?'

'I suppose...' she started, then stopped and took a breath. 'Well...yes,' she finished almost defiantly. 'You could say that. I did—to myself—from time to time.'

'And all the while, I was wondering how in heaven's name to get through to you—badgering my way into your life, spending enormous sums of money, trying to get to know you, to let you know me—anything I could think of to win you over...and it sounds as though I could have done it easily, if I'd only made mad and passionate love to you.'

'I'm not sure it would have been quite as easy as that,' she cautioned.

'Besides, I was holding out for marriage,' he teased, then grew serious again. 'But still, you kept retreating, always so frightened... Your mother's ideas about being a proper young lady and what's attractive—all that had undermined your confidence. And then there was Ralph, and what he did to you. Even without all our other problems, you'd have been a difficult girl to court. It was inevitable—winning you was going to take extreme measures.'

'Which you certainly applied! You kept wearing me down, and I think I must have wanted to be worn down— I *know* I did, but I'd always been so scared. And after Ralph, I decided that the only way not to be hurt was not to get involved, but you just *wouldn't* let me stay uninvolved! I was *sick* when you came through with all that money——'

'But it worked, my love,' he reminded her, pausing long enough to kiss her. 'I told you I was buying time, and it worked.'

'Only barely,' she said tartly, 'and you almost blew it all when you didn't tell me about your company, and then we got here, and I found out. And Leigh was here, and that first evening you were suddenly so distant.'

'I was furious that the whole thing was such a three-ring circus. We'd had such a calm and peaceful time at the shop, and suddenly there was the reality of a business promotion, and I discovered that Carole and Wes had brought Leigh along—one last stand to try to win me back to the fold. I knew it wasn't going to work on me, but I was afraid—terribly afraid—that they would ruin everything for you. For us.

'It was the kind of situation I'd have handled easily, in the old days,' he explained gravely. 'Back when I knew how to be calculating, when nothing mattered very much...but you mattered so much, and I could see things getting worse and worse. You were withdrawing more and more, and I didn't have any idea how to salvage things. I was past the point of even thinking very clearly. I didn't know what to *do*!'

'I think Ralph did it for you,' she offered unsteadily. 'It was shock tactics with a vengeance, but it forced me to *really* think about some things I'd only begun to start thinking about.'

'And I was sure you'd believe him,' Lucas admitted ruefully. 'It would have been in character.'

'But——' she paused, rising up on tiptoe to kiss him quickly, almost shyly '—my character had been changing, all fall long. *You'd* been changing it!'

'And has it changed enough, my love?' he asked, watching her very closely. '*Are* you going to marry me?'

'I've already said I will,' she reminded him, linking her arms around his neck, suddenly prepared—even anxious—to run full tilt into this new world. 'Just tell me when.'

'Tomorrow,' he answered so promptly that it took her breath away. 'Well, not tomorrow, but the day after that. Lord, Jenny! Do you realise what a stroke of luck this is? Where we *are*? That you should agree right now—it's perfect symmetry!'

'Is it?' she asked, smiling up at him, her fingers tangled in his hair. 'What is?'

'Where we are,' he told her, briefly distracted into kissing her again. 'We're in South Carolina,' he resumed with a little effort, 'where, at least in Dillon—which can't be more than thirty or forty miles from here—it only takes twenty-four hours to get married.'

'Does it?' She smiled a dreamy smile, then kissed him back. 'And how would you know that?'

'Years ago, I helped my college room-mate to elope. At the time, I thought he was mad to be in such a rush, but now I know exactly how he feels. We'll check, first thing in the morning—and hope they haven't changed the laws. If they haven't, we'll be married the day after tomorrow.'

'We can't do that,' she objected lazily, because now that everything was so suddenly—miraculously!—settled, a few more days were no hardship. 'First thing in the morning, we've got to get on with the tour.'

'Damn the tour!'

'But we're leading,' she protested. 'We *have* to wait! We can go to Palm Beach and win, and then come back to—where? Dillon?—and get married.'

'No, we'll go to Dillon in the morning,' he insisted. 'Jenny, I've been wanting this since the moment I laid eyes on you, and if you think I'm going to wait a moment longer than absolutely necessary, you're crazy!'

'But the tour——'

'—doesn't matter worth a damn,' he finished for her. 'We're all that matters now!'

When he put it that way, she could hardly object, she conceded. Besides, it was only a little while ago that she'd been thinking that winning the tour was all that mattered to him. *There's* proof that he really loves you, Jen, she told herself, but proof was merely an abstraction now, something she'd stopped needing as soon as she'd taken that grand leap.

'All right. Dillon in the morning,' she agreed, smiling up at him, then couldn't resist a final teasing shot, 'although it does seem a pity, when we're so close to coming in first.'

'We'll come in first the next time...and the next,' he promised between brief kisses. 'We'll have a lifetime full of coming in first.'

There was no arguing with that kind of logic, Jenny decided, so she nodded obediently and kissed him back.

Don't miss one exciting moment of your next vacation with Harlequin's

FREE
FIRST CLASS TRAVEL ALARM CLOCK

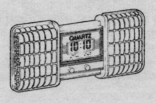

Actual Size
3 ¼ ″ × 1 ¼ ″ h

By reading FIRST CLASS—Harlequin Romance's armchair travel plan for the incurably romantic—you'll not only visit a different dreamy destination every month, but you'll also receive a FREE TRAVEL ALARM CLOCK!

All you have to do is collect 2 proofs-of-purchase from FIRST CLASS Harlequin Romance books. FIRST CLASS is a one title per month series, available from January to December 1991.

For further details, see FIRST CLASS premium ads in FIRST CLASS Harlequin Romance books. Look for these books with the special FIRST CLASS cover flash!

JTLOOK-R

FASHION A WHOLE NEW YOU

WIN
CARS, TRIPS, CASH!

HARLEQUIN®
OFFICIAL SWEEPSTAKES
RULES

NO PURCHASE NECESSARY

1. To enter, complete an Official Entry Form or 3" × 5" index card by hand-printing, in plain block letters, your complete name, address, phone number and age, and mailing it to: Harlequin Fashion A Whole New You Sweepstakes, P.O. Box 9056, Buffalo, NY 14269-9056.

   No responsibility is assumed for lost, late or misdirected mail. Entries must be sent separately with first class postage affixed, and be received no later than December 31, 1991 for eligibility.

2. Winners will be selected by D.L. Blair, Inc., an independent judging organization whose decisions are final, in random drawings to be held on January 30, 1992 in Blair, NE at 10:00 a.m. from among all eligible entries received.

3. The prizes to be awarded and their approximate retail values are as follows: Grand Prize — A brand-new Mercury Sable LS plus a trip for two (2) to Paris, including round-trip air transportation, six (6) nights hotel accommodation, a $1,400 meal/spending money stipend and $2,000 cash toward a new fashion wardrobe (approximate value: $28,000) or $15,000 cash; two (2) Second Prizes — A trip to Paris, including round-trip air transportation, six (6) nights hotel accommodation, a $1,400 meal/spending money stipend and $2,000 cash toward a new fashion wardrobe (approximate value: $11,000) or $5,000 cash; three (3) Third Prizes — $2,000 cash toward a new fashion wardrobe. All prizes are valued in U.S. currency. Travel award air transportation is from the commercial airport nearest winner's home. Travel is subject to space and accommodation availability, and must be completed by June 30, 1993. Sweepstakes offer is open to residents of the U.S. and Canada who are 21 years of age or older as of December 31, 1991, except residents of Puerto Rico, employees and immediate family members of Torstar Corp., its affiliates, subsidiaries, and all agencies, entities and persons connected with the use, marketing, or conduct of this sweepstakes. All federal, state, provincial, municipal and local laws apply. Offer void wherever prohibited by law. Taxes and/or duties, applicable registration and licensing fees, are the sole responsibility of the winners. Any litigation within the province of Quebec respecting the conduct and awarding of a prize may be submitted to the Régie des loteries et courses du Québec. All prizes will be awarded; winners will be notified by mail. No substitution of prizes is permitted.

4. Potential winners must sign and return any required Affidavit of Eligibility/Release of Liability within 30 days of notification. In the event of noncompliance within this time period, the prize may be awarded to an alternate winner. Any prize or prize notification returned as undeliverable may result in the awarding of that prize to an alternate winner. By acceptance of their prize, winners consent to use of their names, photographs or their likenesses for purposes of advertising, trade and promotion on behalf of Torstar Corp. without further compensation. Canadian winners must correctly answer a time-limited arithmetical question in order to be awarded a prize.

5. For a list of winners (available after 3/31/92), send a separate stamped, self-addressed envelope to: Harlequin Fashion A Whole New You Sweepstakes, P.O. Box 4694, Blair, NE 68009.

PREMIUM OFFER TERMS

To receive your gift, complete the Offer Certificate according to directions. Be certain to enclose the required number of "Fashion A Whole New You" proofs of product purchase (which are found on the last page of every specially marked "Fashion A Whole New You" Harlequin or Silhouette romance novel). Requests must be received no later than December 31, 1991. Limit: four (4) gifts per name, family, group, organization or address. Items depicted are for illustrative purposes only and may not be exactly as shown. Please allow 6 to 8 weeks for receipt of order. Offer good while quantities of gifts last. In the event an ordered gift is no longer available, you will receive a free, previously unpublished Harlequin or Silhouette book for every proof of purchase you have submitted with your request, plus a refund of the postage and handling charge you have included. Offer good in the U.S. and Canada only.

HQFW-SWPR

HARLEQUIN® OFFICIAL SWEEPSTAKES ENTRY FORM

4-FWHRS-4

Complete and return this Entry Form immediately – the more entries you submit, the better your chances of winning!

- Entries must be received by **December 31, 1991.**
- A Random draw will take place on **January 30, 1992.**
- No purchase necessary.

Yes, I want to win a FASHION A WHOLE NEW YOU Classic and Romantic prize from Harlequin:

Name _____ Telephone _____ Age _____

Address _____

City _____ State _____ Zip _____

Return Entries to: Harlequin **FASHION A WHOLE NEW YOU,**
P.O. Box 9056, Buffalo, NY 14269-9056   © 1991 Harlequin Enterprises Limited

PREMIUM OFFER

To receive your free gift, send us the required number of proofs-of-purchase from any specially marked FASHION A WHOLE NEW YOU Harlequin or Silhouette Book with the Offer Certificate properly completed, plus a check or money order (do not send cash) to cover postage and handling payable to Harlequin FASHION A WHOLE NEW YOU Offer. We will send you the specified gift.

OFFER CERTIFICATE

Item	A. ROMANTIC COLLECTOR'S DOLL (Suggested Retail Price $60.00)	B. CLASSIC PICTURE FRAME (Suggested Retail Price $25.00)
# of proofs-of-purchase	18	12
Postage and Handling	$3.50	$2.95
Check one	☐	☐

Name _____

Address _____

City _____ State _____ Zip _____

Mail this certificate, designated number of proofs-of-purchase and check or money order for postage and handling to: Harlequin **FASHION A WHOLE NEW YOU Gift Offer,** P.O. Box 9057, Buffalo, NY 14269-9057. Requests must be received by December 31, 1991.

ONE PROOF-OF-PURCHASE   4-FWHRP-4

To collect your fabulous free gift you must include the necessary number of proofs-of-purchase with a properly completed Offer Certificate.

© 1991 Harlequin Enterprises Limited

See previous page for details.